THE LOREKEEPERS: BOOK ONE

RAINE
IN THE UNDERLANDS

CW00972746

Raine in the Underlands The Lorekeepers: Book One © 2023 E M Greville.
All Rights Reserved.

No part of this book may be reproduced in any form or by any electronic or mechanical means including information storage and retrieval systems, without permission in writing from the author. The only exception is by a reviewer, who may quote short excerpts in a review.

This book is a work of fiction. Names, characters, places, and incidents either are products of the author's imagination or are used fictitiously. Any resemblance to actual persons, living or dead, events, or locales is entirely coincidental.

Printed in Australia
Cover design by Shawline Publishing Group Pty Ltd
Illustrations created by Kit Kronk © Playtime Books

Shawline Publishing Group Pty Ltd
www.shawlinepublishing.com.au
First Printing: July 2023

Paperback ISBN 978-1-9229-9346-5
Ebook ISBN 978-1-9229-9357-1

Distributed by Shawline Distribution and Lightning Source Global

A catalogue record for this work is available from the National Library of Australia

More great Shawline titles can be found by scanning the QR code below.
New titles also available through Books@Home Pty Ltd.
Subscribe today at www.booksathome.com.au or scan the QR code below.

THE LOREKEEPERS: BOOK ONE

RAINE
IN THE UNDERLANDS

E M GREVILLE

For my own five monkeys.

CHAPTER 1
A FLYING VISIT

The air crackled and shimmered. A dirty tabby cat with a broken tail sniffed through a bin, ignoring the smell of burned hair wafting over the alley. The tip of its crooked tail was gently smoking, but the cat was unbothered. Perhaps the cat didn't mind. Perhaps cats understood when time and space were in conflict. It howled when an enormous man a long dress and a pointy hat landed on it – so, actually, it did mind. Quite a lot.

The wizard scrambled off and dusted himself down.

'Sorry, Cat,' he said, tossing his tangled black hair over his shoulder.

The wizard wrinkled his bulbous nose and pulled his velvet cloak away from the damp stone walls. Another fizzle and pop; the air bent itself inside out, and a green bag hung upside down like a bat. The cat fled with the rest of its nine lives. The bag dropped to the ground with an 'Oof!' It extended four legs, shook itself like a wet dog and nuzzled the large man's robes.

'Right then. Come on, you.' The wizard crept out from behind the bins. The bag followed close on his heels until it caught the whiff of cat and waddled away down the alley. A shrill whistle soon had it trotting back.

The wizard waggled a sausage finger at the bag. 'Now then, we're supposed to be undercover. You know that, you daft lump. Blending in, that sort of thing. Do you think they have cat-chasing luggage in...?' He held a grubby piece of paper up to the scant light that prodded at the shadows.

The letters glowed and shifted across the paper under the wizard's finger.

'*Scutter's Alley?*'

He tutted and lifted his robes out of a muddy puddle with an empty drink can floating in it. The wizard was distracted by a high-pitched chattering.

TUS'CERTS
LALEY

He took his tall hat, which had *The Magnificent Johnny* embroidered on the brim in fancy gold letters, off his head and turned it upside down, then he reached in and pulled out a squirming monkey. The monkey wasn't an ordinary monkey, even if it did jump up and down on a dustbin and chatter. It was wearing a dirty white T-shirt with 'Sidekick' written on it. The monkey's fur wasn't furry enough, its face was too flat, and its legs were too stumpy. It looked like a mad scientist had taken a toy monkey and brought it life. And then taught it to speak. Which was fairly close to what actually happened.

The wizard listened to the babbling monkey. 'Ah yes, of course. You're absolutely right,' he said.

So, with a flutter of his fingers and a little puff of smoke, the wizard changed out of his wizarding robes. Shabby brown trousers and a scruffy coat were more suitable for a dirty alley in the poor part of town.

The Magnificent Johnny bent down and gave his faithful bag a good old scratch. Blue light danced from Johnny's fingertips. 'Sorry old boy, it's not for long.'

The bag thudded to the ground. It now appeared as just an ordinary bag, stained from years of travel and completely legless. The strange monkey had stopped capering about and sat grumbling on the bin.

Johnny raised his hands like an orchestra conductor about to start a concert.

'Really, Master? Do I have to?' The monkey scratched itself and scowled.

Johnny frowned back. This was serious business. 'You know you have to, Monkey.' Johnny held his breath and sat down on a sturdy bin. The bin groaned. He breathed out slowly. 'Monkey, look at *that*.' Johnny pointed. Splinters of glowing light skittered along the ground. They climbed the walls and fireworks jumped through the air. The lights burst from a hunched figure crouched on the pavement in front of Number Twenty-Six.

'Her Glimmer. I dunno why it's so special. All young witches have the Glimmer.'

'Monkey! Don't you lie to me,' Johnny said.

'Sorry.' Monkey pulled his stumpy, crossed fingers from behind his back. 'It's bigger and brighter than a normal Glimmer. She's special.'

The sky looked like a rainbow had exploded. Puddles of oily blackness oozed after the fragments of colour. One caught up with a spark of light, pounced and devoured it.

'You see that too, don't you?' Johnny whispered.

Monkey nodded. 'Dark energy. Have you seen any Screechers?'

'Not yet, but they won't be far behind. All that dark energy is a picnic for them. She needs someone to watch out for her. She's a halfling. That's why her Glimmer's so bright. If Screechers find her and take her to a Dark One...'

'The end of the worlds?'

The Magnificent Johnny rubbed at his face like it was playdough. 'She needs you, Monkey. We've talked about this. You've got to watch out for her. She's in danger.'

'Why can't you tell her? Then she can learn how to use her powers.'

Johnny shook his head. 'It doesn't work like that. She doesn't know who she is, and it's not up to me to tell her.'

'Well, why can't the Great Elspeta tell her? Why can't *she* look after her?' Monkey demanded.

'Elspeta's a Guardian now. She's banned from magicking. All her power is being used to keep the Gateway shut,' Johnny said. 'You need to watch out for the girl. Not for long. When she's thirteen, she'll be apprenticed. Keep her out of trouble until then.'

'And you promise not to do anything sneaky? Like put a love spell on me?'

Johnny winced. 'No, of course not.' After all, a binding spell wasn't a love spell, was it?

The monkey scowled. 'Well, what about the other bit? You know, the prophecy and all that?'

'Oh, we don't have to worry about that,' Johnny said. 'Elspeta's got the Gateway shut, and the prophecy can only be fulfilled when the gate is opened. By the time anyone works out how to do that, the girl will have her powers under control. It'll be fine.'

He patted the monkey's woolly head. 'Sorry, it won't be for long.'

The monkey took a deep breath, then fell off the bin. He lay still on the pavement – button eyes, wool fur, and a filthy T-shirt. Johnny scooped him up and shoved him in the green bag. He swung the bag over his enormous shoulder and lumbered down the alley to meet the girl huddled outside Number Twenty-Six.

***

Raine's skin prickled. A cold breath whispered past her cheek but the alley was empty, except for a cat crashing about in the bins. Just the wind then. Dark clouds tumbled and chased each other above the crooked rooftops. The sky and her stomach grumbled together. There must be a storm coming. She stirred the puddle at her feet with the toe of her grubby sneaker. The water shone as if someone had poured petrol in it.

She scowled at her reflection. Nope, that didn't work. She couldn't do angry. Not with those big, brown eyes. Cow's eyes, according to Bruiser. No wonder everyone in Scutter's Alley called her Drippy Raine. She'd looked it up in the classroom dictionary after the first time. Then she'd locked herself in the toilets for a good cry. It meant stupid and weak. The only person who didn't call her Drippy Raine was Bruiser, who called her **That Girl**.

Her pointy nose sniffed back at her from the dirty puddle. She wiped it with her sleeve, and ran a bitten fingernailed hand through her hair. Useless. It was like trying to comb a sheep with a spoon. Her arms goose bumped under her baggy jumper.

Behind her loomed the most fallen down house in the poorest street at the wrong end of town. Her house. Her stomach rumbled and tied itself into an empty knot.

Raine squinted in the dusk at a figure stomping up the alleyway. Great. Old Mr Phartz, their landlord. Come to moan about late rent. She could go indoors and get out of the cold but what was the point of giving Bruiser another chance to yell at her?

A round shadow fell across her feet, hiding her reflection. A big man, with a crumpled face and dirty clothes, eased down next to Raine and lay a tattered old bag at his side. He patted it and mumbled, 'Good boy'. But that couldn't be right. People didn't talk to bags.

Raine scooted away, dropping her book into the puddle at her feet with a splash. The man picked it up, shook it and handed it back. She ran her thumb over the smooth cover. Dry. Her skin prickled and the hairs on her arms stood up. Her nose twitched. 'How did you do that?

'You must be Raine. You've got your dad's eyes and your mum's nose,' the man said, as if he hadn't heard her question.

'Who are you?' No one ever talked about her dad, not even Mum. 'What do you know about my dad?'

The man sighed. He scratched a mole on his chin

with a dirty fingernail. 'I didn't know him well, only met him a couple of times. Nice bloke, though.'

Johnny held his hand out. 'Pleased to meet you. I'm an old friend of your mum's. Well, more like family. You can call me Uncle Johnny.'

Raine bit her lip. Should she run away? She wasn't stupid. You didn't last long in a place like Scutter's Alley if you were. Here was a huge, smelly stranger, seeking her out in a deserted street and sitting a bit too close. But he knew her name. And her dad. And he said he was a friend of her mum. Her frazzled little mum didn't have any friends.

'How do you know Mum?'

'We worked together,' Johnny said.

'Doing what?'

'Umm.' The black fingernail crept back up towards the mole. A mole with a hair growing out of it. *Yuck.* 'Sort of security.'

Security? Oh dear. Uncle Johnny was bonkers. But he was more interesting than anyone else she'd spoken to in a while. It beat being inside with Bruiser. Raine held out her hand. It disappeared inside Johnny's.

Burning pinpricks stung her skin as something

hot and itchy reached inside her and tugged, sending her flying up off the pavement. She whizzed past the houses in a speeding blur, the air whooshing out of her lungs as she crashed into a chimney. She wrapped her legs around it, the red bricks digging into her skin through her jeans. She slid and scrabbled for a hole to wedge her fingers in.

Clinging to the chimney, she squinted at the ground below. Who was that down by the road? She couldn't be on the ground and on the roof at the same time, but she could see Uncle Johnny holding her up by the armpits down below. Lights shimmered in the air all around them. The world and her head spun. She gulped. What was happening? Her stomach lurched and rose in her throat. Could she be sick without an actual body? She swallowed and gripped the chimney tighter.

Far below, Uncle Johnny bent over and muttered in her ear. The air sizzled. Raine shot down and thudded back into her body. She opened her eyes. Her fingertips tingled and her head whirled. It felt like the time her school went on a trip to a farm, and she had accidentally touched an electric fence. She stretched out her hand. A flash of blue burst from her fingertips. It streaked over Johnny's head and smashed straight through her front room window.

Oh no! Bruiser! A light snapped on. A furious voice boomed through the shattered window and across the street.

Johnny cursed and pulled open his bag. He glanced at the sky; his head cocked to one side. What was he looking for? Raine stared past him to the window. That was impossible. Wasn't it? She wiggled her fingers. Only one way to find out. Johnny lunged, closing his fist around her hand.

'No!' he snapped. 'You can't do that here!' He scrabbled around in the bag next to him. He pulled out an old, dirty toy and threw it in Raine's lap.

Lights flickered on all down Scutter's Alley. It wouldn't be long before everyone was leaning out of their doorways to see what was going on. Then she'd be in for it.

Johnny stood up and dusted off his trouser legs. He bent over Raine. 'This is Monkey. He was your mum's. Then he was mine. Now he's yours. You need to look after him, and he'll look after you.'

Raine poked the toy. Johnny grabbed her hand and pressed the monkey into her grip. Electricity sparked between them, hot and sharp. He was telling the truth. *I can feel it. I trust you.* She picked up the monkey and held it as far away as she could.

It might survive a hot wash. Then she could stick it on a shelf in her room. Hidden behind something a bit less childish.

The door to Number Twenty-Six crashed open.

'Bruiser! Mum!' Raine yelped.

Bruiser stood framed in the doorway. A hulking figure in a stained vest; his muscled, tattooed forearms stretched out to his sides. His long, hairy fingers curled around the door as if he was about to rip it from its hinges. Elsie, Raine's mother, peeked around from behind him like a mouse round a pit bull.

Bruiser thumped out onto the cracked pavement. Johnny was nowhere to be seen – he had gone, his bag with him. Raine clutched the toy in her arms. Bruiser would try and take it. He always ruined everything. But Uncle Johnny had given it to her for a reason, whatever that might be. *It's mine.* She raised her chin and glared.

Curtains twitched all down the street. No one dared come out and complain when Bruiser was around. Her mum sneaking under Bruiser's arm, squealed and clamped a hand over her mouth. She scanned the sky.

Bruiser grabbed Raine by the shoulder, shaking

her so hard her teeth clacked together. 'What's this?' he snarled, trying to tear the monkey from her hand.

'Get off me!' Raine yelled. She sank her teeth into Bruiser's hand. He growled like a bear and shook Raine so hard her shoe fell off and landed in the puddle. She kicked him. Her bare toes connected with his shin, sending shockwaves up her leg. Fire flashed in her toe. Had she ripped a nail off? He roared. She held on tight to the monkey. Bruiser wasn't getting his hands on it.

Gripping Raine's shoulder tight enough to make the bones crunch together, Bruiser thundered into the house with Elsie clinging to him.

'Stop!' Raine's mother pleaded. Elsie clawed at Bruiser's back, hanging off him like an extra coat. He stormed down the damp hall towards the kitchen, dragging Raine with him.

'That girl can sit and think about what she's done! That window will have to be paid for!' Bruiser opened a door and flung Raine inside.

She slid down a flight of wooden stairs and smashed through a stack of cardboard boxes. The door slammed behind her. Bruiser didn't bother locking it. Raine crouched in a ball, the toy monkey cradled in her arms. No way she was going to cry.

Not about Bruiser. *I can't believe I bit him! And kicked him!* Whatever had got into Drippy Raine? She'd never done anything like that before. She buried her face into its matted, grubby fur. The monkey felt warm, like a hot water bottle. It did stink a bit though.

CHAPTER 2
NO ORDINARY WALL

Raine was used to finding herself shut in the gloomy basement awaiting her punishment. She crept around toppling piles of old newspapers written in a language her mum said was Dutch. Inching towards the frayed light cord hanging from the cobwebbed bare bulb, she stretched up on tiptoes and pulled it. Flickering, dim light filled the little room.

She put out a hand to steady herself.

Raine's palm itched. The letters under her hand twisted and scurried around like black spiders under her hand.

Well, *that* had never happened before. She scooped the paper up and held it in front of her eyes. Gobbledygook. It was a trick of the dim light. But for a second, the words had made sense. What had they said? She scratched her head. Why couldn't she remember?

She plopped the paper back. Men who talk to bags, out of body experiences, finger flames, and moving words. Her brain thumped against her skull. It was too small to keep all her thoughts in. It pounded against her eyes. Mum always said 'curiosity killed the cat' whenever Raine asked about the stuff in the basement. Which was a bit stupid, because Raine wasn't a cat – but maybe it wasn't worth thinking about too deeply. Grown-ups said weird things all the time. She should sit down and wait for Bruiser to let her out.

A pop sounded above her head as the lightbulb went out, plunging Raine into darkness. Great. Although, at least if it was dark, she wouldn't be able to see any other impossible things.

She'd spent enough time in there over the years to know where everything was. She might as well get comfortable.

Raine pulled out an old rug covered in faded

embroidery and draped it around her shoulders. A cloud of dust rose from its stiff folds and she sneezed. The golden stitching flared. *Stop it!* Her eyes were playing tricks in the dark.

She snuggled up with Monkey in her arms. He wasn't as smelly as she'd first thought. He was cute. Why did she feel so connected to this bedraggled, old toy? Maybe because it was as tattered and ragged as her.

Sitting in the dark was even more boring than being stuck outside. Raine stroked Monkey's matted fur. She supposed she could pass the time by telling him stories. Mum had told Raine some fantastic tales of distant worlds and magical creatures, but Raine preferred her own made-up adventures. Especially the ones about herself and her real dad battling evil and living happily ever after.

A voice danced around her brain. Who was this mysterious Uncle Johnny? What didn't she know about her mum? What had happened when that blue flame had shot out of her finger? And why did it feel it so important to look after this battered toy? Her head swam. Too many questions and no answers. She closed her eyes. She breathed in slowly through her nose and out through her mouth, the way Mrs

Placidus had taught her class in school when Jim and Tommy had a fight.

***

A rustling noise woke Raine. She opened her eyes and clapped a hand over her mouth. Something glowed greenish yellow on Monkey's head. Raine dropped the monkey with a yelp, and a tiny creature flew into the air.

'Sorry!' it squeaked, 'I didn't mean to scare you!'

'Wha... wh... um... uh!' Raine shook her head. 'I mean, what... Did you speak, or did I imagine that too? Maybe Bruiser shook me a bit too hard.'

The little animal giggled and fluttered its wings. It hovered before Raine. In the glow that shone from its body, she stared at its tiny, horse-like head with a horn above its nose, green scales like a crocodile, and a long tail with a sharp point at the end. She blinked. Still there. It kept itself in the air by flapping bat-like wings tipped with needle claws. A sickly light flickered in its belly, where the green scales faded to a pale yellow. It stared back. Bruiser must have shaken her *really* hard.

'I'm lost, you know!' it gulped and then burped.

The glow in its belly flared, and two plumes of grey smoke shot out of its nostrils.

Raine coughed and her eyes watered. Rotten eggs. And she'd thought Monkey was smelly!

'I got in here, and I don't remember how, and now I don't know how to get home!' It flapped closer to Raine's face. 'I'm only little. Mum says I'll always be her baby.'

Raine laughed. The giant fist that had been squeezing her chest let go. *I'm more frightened of Bruiser than I am of this tiny thing.* She smiled and held out her hand. The little beast flew to her and stood up on its hind legs. It folded its wings over its back and burped again. Its tummy brightened. The horrible smell hit her in the face. Raine wrinkled her nose. The bug reminded her of something, but that was impossible, unless it was a mutant firefly.

'Where have you come from?' she asked.

The creature rubbed its wings together. 'I'm not sure. I was with my friends, and we were having a competition to see who could glow the brightest. But it wasn't dark enough, so I flew off. I flew up, and up, and then suddenly I was *here!*'

'Don't worry, we'll find your way home,' Raine said.

'Promise?'

She nodded. 'Promise. No matter what.' She cupped the creature in her hand, scurried up the stairs and eased open the door.

Bruiser's raging voice filled the small space. *'I'll find it one day, Elsie! You can't keep me here forever!'*

The creature jumped up and down on Raine's hand. 'Not there! Not there! It's bad out there! Everyone says so!'

'I'm sorry. I didn't know.' Raine held her hand up and looked into its tiny eyes. 'Well, that's not true. I do know it's bad out there, but I didn't know anyone else knew. Anyway, who is "everyone"?'

'I don't know.' A trail of water trickled down the creature's face. It sniffed back its tears, and its glow dimmed for a moment. 'I'm only little. Everyone. My mum says. She says the Dark One will take our fire away forever if we don't behave! She'd kill me if she thought I went out there!'

Dark One? That couldn't be good. Was Bruiser the Dark One? The world tilted under her feet. She sat on the top step with a thunk. Who was more afraid, Drippy Raine or this little creature?

Time to stop being Drippy Raine. It needed her help. She squared her shoulders. If only she could stop her hands trembling and her legs shaking.

'Alright. You didn't come in through the door. So how did you get in? You said you flew up and up, so where can you have come from?'

'I don't know. I'm only little.'

'Let me think. If you didn't come in through the door, there must be a hole somewhere. But you're tiny, how are we going to find it?'

'I don't know! I'm only—'

'Yes, yes,' Raine interrupted, 'you're only little.' She clicked her fingers. 'I know! Come here, little one, I'll need your light for this.'

The animal flew up to Raine's face and hovered in front of her. It held out a wing, its claw outstretched. 'Pleased to meet you, but my name's not Little One, it's Little Thirty-Five. Little One's my big brother.'

'Well, it's very nice to meet you, Little Thirty-Five.' Raine held out her finger to the animal's claw and gently shook it. 'My name's Raine.'

'Rain?' Little Thirty-Five looked her up and down. 'What a funny name.'

'Well, you're a number.'

'I'm not *just* a number. Mum says I'm special.'

'Hmmm. Can you make that light in you any brighter?'

Little Thirty-Five nodded. 'I think so.' He swallowed a huge breath and burped. His belly flickered bright yellow. He snorted a final effort, and a flash of orange flame burst from his bottom.

'Ow! Ow!' Little Thirty-Five cried dancing up and down, flapping his wings behind him. 'My botty!'

He calmed down and stopped flapping. Was he smiling?

'You look pleased with yourself, Little Thirty-Five.'

He puffed out his chest. 'I didn't know I could do that. Since she cursed us, we have fire in our bellies that we can't breathe out. I didn't know I could fart my fire out!'

Raine pointed to a corner where the floor and wall met. 'I think I saw something, down there!' She shuffled down the stairs.

Little Thirty-Five flew down, turned away from the corner and lifted his tail. He grunted, and a small flame shot out, lighting up a hole between the wall and the floorboards. Raine put her hand in it and waggled her fingers. Where was the floor? Little Thirty-Five edged up to the hole, then backed away from it.

How could there be no floor? The neighbours' house should be on the other side of the wall. It must mean she'd found a way to get her strange little friend home. She stuck her hand through the hole. Nothing. She pulled her hand back out, but the ragged sleeve of her jumper got snagged.

She was stuck. Raine pulled as hard as she could. A crack zigzagged right down the middle of the wall. But she wasn't free. Something on the other side of the wall held her there. Her stomach clenched. A hot ball rose in her throat. She swallowed, but it wouldn't go away.

***

Far below the basement, a hooded figure stood in a dark forest, on top of a hill. Its face was raised to the sky. Its arms were outstretched, its fingers bent. A speck of blue appeared high in the night sky, quickly stretching to become a glowing line that split the darkness with a crack like thunder. The treetops rustled and exploded with winged shadows twisting and turning through the sky. The figure grinned up at the jagged tear in the sky. Soon it would take the halfling's Glimmer. Its fingers straightened, and its hands dropped to its sides.

***

Raine wrenched with all her might. Her sleeve tore free, and she crashed to the floor, landing flat on her back. She pulled Monkey out from underneath her. Little Thirty-Five circled her head. She lifted herself onto her elbows and looked at the wall. It didn't look *right.* She couldn't put her finger on what it was; there was something *wrong* about it. Last Christmas, Raine had been given the part of Stable Door in her school's nativity play. She'd had to wear a massive piece of cardboard with a hole cut in it for her face. This wall looked equally as unconvincing, but less embarrassed.

Bruiser always said she was a nosy little bleeder; her mum said she was naturally curious. Raine shrugged. It didn't matter who was right. She kicked the wall. It wobbled, which wasn't very wall-like at all. She shuffled forward until she was kneeling in front of it. Gripping the wall around the crack, she tugged hard. A piece of plaster came away in her hand. It looked like wall. She sniffed it, but it didn't smell of paint, like she thought a wall should. It smelt *bad*, like Bruiser's dirty socks which he stuffed down the back of the sofa instead of putting in the washing basket. Raine gagged and threw the plaster away, narrowly missing Little Thirty-Five, who was peering out from behind her shoulder. She tugged at the rest of the wall.

Raine started to rip a hole in the so-called wall. It crumbled. There was no way it could be real. It was like someone had put a screen up to hide something. But to hide what? What was on the other side? A shiver tickled her spine. She laid Monkey in her lap. That was better.

Raine tore handfuls of plaster away. Little Thirty-Five weaved about, landing on her shoulder and rubbing his wings together.

'It *is* the right way!' he shouted in his high-pitched warble, an excited kettle whistling in her ear. 'I remember now! I recognise the other side! My friends must all be round there!'

Eventually, Raine had torn a hole big enough to squeeze through. She tucked Monkey under her arm and peered through the opening. Nothing. A big, black emptiness. Little Thirty-Five whizzed past her and into the darkness.

'Little Thirty-Five!' she called. Her voice echoed back to her. Little Thirty-Five must have found his way home. His glow had vanished. She squinted in the gloom. If only she had a torch.

Raine lay down on her stomach and crawled forward. She gripped the edge of the floor on her side of the house. No good. She might as well have her eyes shut. She slid forward. The floor groaned. Raine slipped closer to the edge. She shuffled back, but bits of the floor came away and plummeted down into the darkness.

Her feet scrabbled and slipped on the shrinking piece of floor she clung to. It tilted further down. She grabbed at the wall. Monkey slid down the floor, caught on a jagged splinter, and hung over the edge.

She lunged. The floor groaned and collapsed, plunging into the darkness. Raine's fingers scrabbled at the rough wall. The toy spiralled away into the dark. Her aching fingers slipped. She kicked out with her legs. If only they would connect with something. *Anything!* But there was nothing. She hung in space.

'Monkey!' she cried. 'Help me, Monkey!'

She wasn't going to get help from a toy. But perhaps someone might hear her – even if it was Bruiser. This was not turning out like one of her stories at all.

She clambered higher. Her fingertips clawed at the wall. Her arms felt as though they were being wrenched from their sockets. Her shoulder muscles screamed at her to let go.

Whoosh.

Raine froze.

What was that noise? There it was again. And again. It was getting closer. Her shoulders burned, her fingertips bled. She spotted something glowing in the distance.

'Little Thirty-Five! Help! Go back and get help before I fall!' she yelled.

It must be Little Thirty-Five coming towards her. But he didn't stop. 'Quickly! Before it's too late! I can't hold on much longer!'

He powered through the darkness. He looked much bigger than he had looked in the cupboard. *I don't think that's Little Thirty-Five.*

Its green light burned brighter and sicklier – like a jar of fluorescent bogies. Its leathery wings, with razor-sharp talons, propelled it up through the air like a shark swimming through water. Her heart hammered. Sweat trickled down her back.

The monster rocketed up. It chomped its jaws open and shut with a snap. Raine dangled inches above rows of deadly sharp teeth. She pulled her legs up. The monster growled.

Snap! Snap!

If she let go now, she would be eaten. Her raw fingers fumbled against the wall. Her sweat made it slippery. She couldn't grasp it. She slid down. *No!* She clutched at the edge. It snapped off under her hand. She dangled by one arm. Her hand slipped.

Snap! Snap!

She clutched at nothing. Too late. She fell.

Whomp!

The creature slammed into her like a train.

'Please don't hurt me!' she wheezed.

The monster ignored her. It tore its horn through the back of her jumper.

'Don't...' it growled.

A chunk of wall slammed into Raine's forehead. The world went black.

CHAPTER 3
HERE BE MONSTERS

Were those voices? Raine kept her eyes shut. She must have fainted. Where was she? Her fingers brushed something soft under her. The monster? What if it had eaten her and she was lying in its stomach? Like that boy and the whale in the story Mrs Placidus had read to her class.

Panic rose like a wave. She was going to drown in it. Raine tried to breathe like Mrs Placidus said, but the air got stuck in her throat. She gasped and coughed. Snot shot out of her nose.

'Ew!'

Raine opened one eye a fraction and peered through her lashes. Little Thirty-Five hovered in front of her face.

'She's awake! She's awake!' he squeaked in his loudest squeak.

'Ssh!' Raine shook her head. *No, no, no!*

'What for? My brother rescued you!' Little Thirty-Five bobbed up and down.

She flexed her arms, but they were stuck to her sides. She kicked her legs, but they were tied down. Tears welled and followed the trail of snot down her face. She couldn't even wipe it off.

'How can I be safe if I'm tied up in a—' Raine looked around her prison. 'In a bedroom?' The painted ceiling soared above her head. 'My whole house could fit in here.' She squinted. 'I hate pink.'

'Don't let Mum hear you say that!' Little Thirty-Five squealed, fluttering around in front of a window framed in pink velvet curtains that matched the wallpaper. One wall was covered in framed photos of the thing that had attacked her. In some it wore make-up and jewellery, and others it had a beard, or glasses.

Mum? Brother?

'Did you say your *brother* rescued me? I thought he was going to eat me!'

Little Thirty-Five giggled. He pointed with his

tiny claw to the first picture in the top row, which depicted a monster with stubble on its green face. 'Him. Little One. He saved you.' He pointed to the next picture: a red monster with a pearl necklace. 'That's Little Two, my biggest sister.' He flew down to the very last picture, a small portrait. 'That's me!'

'They're all your brothers and sisters?'

'Yep!'

'How many of you are there?'

'Thirty-five.'

'Your parents named you numbers?'

'No, not really. We've got proper names, but no one ever uses them.'

He buzzed away out the door while Raine was still gawking at the portraits.

A thumping sound echoed around the room. She jumped. What was it? A pile of flowery pillows blocked her view. It couldn't be footsteps; it was way too loud.

What was that noise? A buzzing near her head. And a smell. Little Thirty-Five flew up and down near her ear.

'I told my mum you're awake! Here she is!'

Raine looked up. And up. The eyes of a nightmare glowered down at her. She cowered against the cushions. She tried to swallow but her throat was too dry.

'Alright, my love. I expect you've had a bit of a shock. You lie still now and try to take it easy. No hurry now, is there?' The monster's voice was soft and kind. Raine blinked and stopped trying to hide in the pillows. Monsters weren't supposed to talk like that! Monsters were supposed to say things like 'Gggrrr.'

It stood up on thick, scaled back legs. The claws wrapped around a hot, steaming cup were painted pale pink. Green wings furled neatly against its back. The monster wore a kitchen apron with "World's Best Mum" written on it.

'That's my mum!' Little Thirty-Five said.

Raine licked her dry lips. She peeled her tongue from the roof of her mouth. 'That's *your* mum?' Her voice squeaked out as high as Little Thirty-Five's.

'I'm his mum,' the monster agreed. 'You can call me Flo, my darlin'.'

Flo put the cup down onto the bedside table and loosened the covers around Raine. So *that* was why she couldn't move. She'd been tucked in too tight, not tied up. Using a pink tissue, the monster wiped the snot and tears away from Raine's face, brushing her hair back. Flo sat down on the edge of the bed.

'I expect you're wondering what's going on, dear. It's not often we get visitors from the other side. Not since they shut the door, anyway.' Flo paused, picked up the mug and passed it to Raine. She gripped it in both hands.

'Here you are, love. Drink this. It'll help you feel a bit more normal.'

The liquid was a thick, dark red. Her stomach churned at the sight of it.

Flo laughed, a deep rumble that shook the bed. Little Thirty-Five buzzed around the mug. His mum swatted him away.

'Don't worry, ducky,' the monster said, 'it's not blood! We're vegetarians. It's betelnut tea. It'll give you your strength back in no time!' Flo stood up, straightened her apron, and belched. Two plumes of stinky smoke poured from her nostrils and wrapped themselves around Raine's head. Her eyes watered.

'Pardon me. Terrible heartburn today. That awful witch has a lot to answer for! Now, you drink that up like a good girl, and I'll come back and see how you're doing later. I'm sure your poor little head's spinning, so you get that down.'

Raine thanked Flo before she left. They might look scary, but the monsters had saved her life. It was time to stop calling them monsters. Mum always said appearances could be deceiving. Turns out she was right. Raine examined the pictures on the wall. There was something about them. She frowned. They couldn't be familiar; it was impossible.

Raine blew on the tea and took a sip. *Yum!* She gulped it down. It helped. Little Thirty-Five flittered around the bed for a bit.

'Well, see you later!' he said.

'Hang on!' Raine said, 'Thank you for sending your brother to rescue me!'

Little Thirty-Five hovered by the bedroom door. 'I didn't. I just came home.'

'But then, how did he know I needed rescuing?'

'Your monkey told us,' he said. Raine spat a mouthful of red tea all over the bed spread. Little Thirty-Five seemed not to notice, and disappeared through the open door.

Her hands shook and she fumbled the mug as she placed it onto the bedside table. Raine rubbed at the mess, her mind backing away like a timid animal when it came too close to thinking about what Little Thirty-Five had said. The pitter-patter of little feet crossed the bedroom floor. *It can't be. It's a toy.*

'I wouldn't worry about that.' The voice came from near her feet. 'Flo's a pretty dab hand with all that cleaning stuff. We've got other things to worry about.'

'Oh.' Raine stared hard at the bedspread, avoiding looking at the toy. 'You're real now, are you?'

'Yup. Look, you'll have to get used to it sometime, so you might as well get it over with.'

'Okay.' She held her breath and peeked at the toy.

Monkey gave a cheerful wave with one of his furry brown paws. Stubby arms folded over his chest as she gawked at him. He wore a grubby T-shirt which was stretched over a fat tummy and brown eyes – not buttons, but *real* eyes. Which was all impossible, because Monkey was just a toy. Or so she had thought.

'Not so bad, is it?'

'Ummm...' At least she was already lying down. How many times in one day could a person feel like fainting?

Monkey stuck his tongue out and a giggle popped like a bubble out of Raine. He scampered over and threw himself at Raine, kissed her on the cheek and wrapped his arms around her neck. She squeezed him. Phew! He smelled like a real monkey too.

'Mum must've hugged you a lot,' Raine whispered. 'It feels like getting a hug from her.' Monkey went stiff in her arms, and she let go of him. 'Sorry.'

Monkey picked at his fur. Did he have fleas or was he cross with her? Why? He had been her mum's toy, after all.

'I'm... I mean... What's happening?' Raine snorted back tears. She could hear Mum's voice in her head telling her off.

Monkey gave her a little smile, but it didn't reach his eyes.

'Well,' he said, 'you like telling stories, don't you? And your mum, bet she's told you some cracking stories.'

What did Monkey know about Mum? And why did everyone suddenly think her little, boring, mum was so interesting?

'Your stories are full of magic, aren't they?'

Raine nodded.

'So is life. You've got to look for it. Or sometimes it finds you. Some people attract magic, whether they want to or not. Not often in your world – but you're different.'

'But I wasn't looking for magic! And what do you mean, "my world"?'

Monkey patted Raine's arm. 'You've been looking for magic all your life. I think it was looking for you this time.'

Heat rushed up Raine's body. The room spun. She kicked off the covers. 'What are you talking about? What magic?'

Monkey shook his head. 'Life would be much easier if magic wasn't always interfering, sticking its nose in, and upsetting everyone's plans. None of this is supposed to happen until you're in control. But no, the magic came sniffing around and watch out, next thing we've fallen through a hole in the world and come out on the other side. Typical. I should be having a much nicer time somewhere else, yet here we are.'

'Looking for *me*? But why?' She didn't believe it. Nothing ever happened to her.

'Because you're one of the important ones. The most important one in this world.'

Why was it so hot in here? Tears stung Raine's eyes. What was her toy talking about? No, he wasn't a toy. Toys couldn't move and speak. A *friend*, that's what Monkey was, and she needed a friend, even if he was talking nonsense.

Before she asked any important questions, she'd start with a little question. One that didn't really matter. Then, if Monkey said something that made any sense at all, she would ask something more urgent, like, 'WHAT IS GOING ON?'

She breathed deeply. Mrs Placidus would be proud. 'So, how were you made?'

'It's magic, isn't it? It's always magic, everything. You'll learn that. My maker harnessed the magic and *poof!* Here I am. I was made by a very powerful wizard. One of the most powerful in all the worlds. You met him. Uncle Johnny.'

The enormous man with the shadows under his eyes, old clothes, and wobbly chins?

'Uncle Johnny? Didn't look much like a powerful wizard to me. I thought wizards had long beards and pointy hats and wore dresses.'

'In some worlds he does. I know you've got loads of questions, but we don't have time. And anyway, I'm not the one to answer them all. I'm just a witch's... a friend.' Monkey shrugged as if Raine should know what he meant. He sighed at her blank stare. 'It'll have to wait.' He leaped off the bed. 'I'll go and tell the Council you're nearly ready.'

Monkey jumped to the door. 'Don't worry! I'm here to help you all I can. Johnny wasn't lying when he said what a good friend I am.' He skipped out of the room. Raine sagged back against the pillows. Her brain tumbled about in her skull like dirty sneakers in a washing machine. She rubbed the heels of her hands into her eyes until stars danced behind her lids. This all had to be a dream.

An enormous green head poked itself round the bedroom door. It leered at Raine, all teeth and drool. Not a dream then, more like a nightmare. She rubbed her eyes again. Flo came into the room.

'It's only me, my lovely!' Flo said. Her lipsticked mouth was snagged on curved, pointed tooth. Raine's heart stopped trying to leap out of her chest. Flo was smiling, not leering. Her tooth had a smear of bright pink lipstick on it.

Flo walked over to the bed; red material folded over her arm and a huge silver jug in her hand. Settling down beside her, she patted Raine's hand. 'Look, my ducky, it's alright. You're among friends here. I know we might not be much to look at, but we'll do you no harm!'

Raine's cheeks burned. Had she been that obvious?

'Now, let's be having you, pet.' Flo whipped back the bedding covering Raine, who quickly drew her knees up to her chest.

'Flo! Where are my clothes?' Raine's cheeks were on fire. 'Who undressed me?'

'Why I did my pet, of course! Ripped right through, from collar to cuff they was. And covered in, well I don't know what, I hate to think where you've been playing! Seen it all before too, so don't you worry about that! I was the princelings' nurse, you know! Scrawny little things, same as you, they were. Come on then, you little stick insect! I undressed you, and now I'll bathe you and then I'll dress you. In *this*.'

Flo shook out the cloth she had been carrying. Raine gaped at a pair of red, velvet trousers covered in delicate silver embroidery, matched with a tunic in the same material. Her fingers itched to stroke them.

'That's for me? Really for me?' She reached out and touched the top with her fingertip while Flo bustled about with the jug. Scented steam floated up from a metal bath at Flo's feet.

'Of course it's for you!' Flo burped out a waft of smoke. Thank goodness the steam masked the smell.

'My orders were to make a suit that could be gone adventuring in, so here it is. Did it while you were asleep, I did. Ooh, this fell down with you too.' She handed Raine a tan bag. She glimpsed her old book inside.

Raine jumped down from the high bed, rolling to break her fall. She threw her arms around the creature.

'Thank you,' she whispered into Flo's tummy.

'Well, now,' Flo said, 'best be getting you in this bath, eh? Can't have you turning up to see The Grand Council covered in muck, can we? Whatever have you been doing? You look like you've been rolling around in a bag of flour.' Raine looked down at her hands and arms which were still covered in plaster dust and cobwebs. 'Proper little urchin, you are.' She curled her pink painted talons around Raine and plonked her in a tub of hot, perfumed water.

CHAPTER 4
A MEETING OF MINDS

Her hair clean and brushed for once, Raine crept from the bedroom. She ran a finger over the leather bag and hooked the long strap over her head. Her mum's book thumped against her thigh. She straightened the hem of her red tunic.

'So pretty. Amazing,' she said, admiring the fabric.

'Yes, well, she's got a thing for royalty, hasn't she?' said Monkey, who was walking a few paces behind, grumbling under his breath and tugging at his fancy red waistcoat. He scowled and pulled on a pair of suede gloves. 'Honestly, I feel like my friend, the white rabbit. It's embarrassing.'

Raine stopped and turned on her heel. 'What is embarrassing, Monkey?'

The little primate flapped a glove at his waistcoat. 'All this *drama*,' he snorted. 'Totally ridiculous and unnecessary. We've got a job to do, and we should do it! Do you realise how much time we *don't* have?'

Raine shook her head.

'Exactly,' he continued, 'neither do I. That's the whole point, no one does. And where's my T-shirt? I bet Flo'll wash it, even though I told her not to. I hate it when it's clean! Have to get it dirty all over again! And this horrid outfit too. I look stupid.'

They were walking down a long stone corridor. At intervals along the wall, flaming torches spluttered in front of long tapestries hanging against the rock. Raine paused at one of the wall hangings, coughing up a lungful of torch smoke. She wheezed at a tapestry of two figures; one short and dressed in red, the other tall with long, black hair snaking around her head. Tongues of flame shot from their fingers.

Raine touched a curl already escaping out of her tight plait and fingered the material of her new suit. Monkey was busy pulling on a loose seam at the hem of his waistcoat and tapping his foot.

'Is there any point in asking what on earth's going on?' she asked.

'No, but the quicker we get there, the quicker you'll find out. So, come on!'

Tugging on Raine's hand, he led her to the end of the passage. It opened out into an enormous stone room. Rows of tents and stalls had been set up. Hundreds of creatures – green, red and purple – ambled around the hall. Some huge like Flo, others like Little Thirty-Five, and all sizes in between. On a stage at the far end of the room, a rainbow beast juggled while another strummed a guitar. The creatures were dressed in flowing silks and velvets, sparkling with mirrors, sequins and baubles that flashed in the light. Music drifted across the room.

Raine ducked into the tunnel. She peeked back around the corner. She'd seen these creatures before, but how? *What are they?*

Outside the tents, heaped tables gleamed with jewellery and sparkling gems. Raine resisted the urge to dive in and let the stones trickle through her fingers. Other tables groaned under bolts of brightly dyed cloth.

Monkey whispered, 'It's a fiesta. A festival. And no, it's not always like this. Yes, it is a special occasion.' Raine opened her mouth, but Monkey cut her off. 'And yes, it is because you're here. And no, I can't tell you why!'

Spices filled the air. A waft of roasting garlic drifted straight under Raine's nose. She breathed it in. Her stomach grumbled like thunder. The familiar heat rose in her face. Great. No one would be able to tell where her clothes ended, and her face began.

The room hushed. Hundreds of pairs of eyes swivelled to look at Raine. Her face couldn't get any hotter, but it tried.

Monkey pulled Raine back into the corridor. 'Right. This is it then. Stay behind me and don't stop.'

Monkey strode into the room. The creatures dropped before him, their wings sweeping the ground. Raine scurried along behind him, weaving through bowing bodies and jumping over creatures lying in front of her, covering their heads with their wings. Were they ever going to get through the crowd? It was like doing hurdles on sports day. Raine wiped sweat from her eyes. *Finally.* She hopped over the last beast. Monkey slowed down to walk by her side.

'Well done.' He squeezed her hand.

'What now?' Raine held her palm up to her burning cheek. She could cook an egg on it.

Monkey pointed a paw upwards. 'Your carriage awaits you, Ma'am!'

Raine ducked. '*What's that?*' she squealed, hiding behind her hands.

The biggest of the creatures she'd seen hovered above their heads. A golden saddle gleamed on its back. The animal landed and bowed in front of Raine, its head to the floor.

'At your service, Your Highness,' it rumbled. It kept its enormous horn pressed to the ground.

What was it doing? Why didn't it get up? Monkey nudged Raine and lifted his chin. *Oh.*

'Please, do get up!' What now? She reached out and patted the animal on its shoulder.

'I'm very sorry if I scared you earlier, Ma'am,' the creature said, its head still bowed. 'Didn't know it was you. Didn't want you to fall, see? Wasn't till Mum told me I found out! Such an honour, Ma'am. Thank you!'

This must be Little One, Flo's son. He'd saved her when she fell out of the basement.

'It's me who should be thanking you, Little One! You saved my life! If there's anything I can ever do for you... And, please, don't call me Ma'am. My name's Raine. You are Little One, aren't you?' Was she handling this right? If no one would tell her what *this* was, it wasn't her fault if she got it wrong, was it?

Was he crying? She'd messed up. The beast sniffed and burped. A cloud of deadly smelling smoke enveloped her.

'I'm your humble servant – Little One. I would die for you, my lady.' Perhaps she hadn't messed up after all. What a strange thing to say though. Her heart fluttered and skipped. *It's fine. It's only a saying.*

Little One sank to his belly. Monkey gestured to the seat on his back, and Raine scrambled up the gold rope ladder swinging down Little One's side. She sat back against soft purple cushions. Monkey scrabbled up beside her and tapped the front of the saddle. Little One beat his wings, and they soared into the air.

Little One flew upwards in a spiral. Round holes marked the walls, as if animals had burrowed their way through the rock.

'That's exactly what it is,' Monkey said.

Did he read her thoughts? She stared at him. Monkey shrugged. He seemed a lot more relaxed now they were on their way. Squirming against the cushions, he waved a paw at the stone walls.

'Burrows,' he said. 'This is the Hive. Where they live, work, eat and play. Clawed out of the rock by the first generation.'

'Generation of what?'

Monkey flicked his paw in Little One's direction, 'Him. And the others, of course.'

'But what are they, I mean.'

Why wouldn't Monkey answer any of her questions? Raine's head throbbed and her nerves blazed. Nothing made sense. Even her thigh, where her bag rested, burned.

Monkey sighed. 'So many questions, Raine. You sound like your mum. Shame you don't have a guidebook or something, isn't it?'

Raine's nostrils twitched. What was that smell?

'Argh!' She jumped up in the saddle, slapping at her leg. 'I'm on fire! Monkey! Help!'

'No, you're not. Calm down.' Monkey pointed at her leg. 'Look.'

He was right. Of course there were no flames or smoke, that would be crazy. Raine sat back down, careful not to get a glimpse over the edge of the saddle at the long drop below. But her leg was boiling hot. She lifted the bag up off her lap. She yelped.

'It's the bag! It's burning me!' Raine puffed out her cheeks and blew on the bag.

Monkey crossed his arms. 'Um, what are you doing?'

'Cooling it down!'

'Why?'

'Because it's burning!' Was Monkey always this annoying?

Monkey sighed, as if *she* was the annoying one! 'No, Raine, *why* is hot? Do your bags often turn into ovens while you're wearing them?'

'Well. I suppose not.' Raine held the bag at arms-length. She prodded it. 'It's cooling down.' She lifted the flap and peered inside.

'It's *this*!' Raine pulled out her battered old paperback book. She turned it over and held it out to Monkey. 'It's different!'

The book wasn't old anymore. It looked brand-new. The cover was soft blue leather; warm like skin, as if the book was alive. Curly gold letters crossed the front and ran down the spine. Raine squinted at the ornate writing:

'I'm sure it wasn't called that before,' she muttered. 'It used to be *Imagined Lands and Fairy Tales*. And it had a big stain on it.'

The book fell open to a coloured picture. A boy stood in front of a castle. In the air above him two creatures, one red and one white, battled each other. Raine's finger traced the writing under the drawing:

She pointed at Little One and back at the book. 'True tales? He's one of *these*?' She tapped the red dragon on the page. 'And Flo, and Little Thirty-Five, and all of them? Dragons?'

Monkey nodded.

'Huh.'

Dragons were *real*. She should be more surprised than she was. But weren't dragons supposed to breathe fire? There must be something wrong with them – that was why they kept doing those disgusting smoke burps.

'They live here? In this Hive?'

'Yep. Western Dragons. They used to store all the gold they collected here. The place was full. But then the witch cursed them – took their fire and stole all their gold. Now they live here, in the Hive, instead.'

'Who is this witch?' Raine asked. 'Flo said she has a lot to answer for.'

'We get off in a minute. Enjoy the view!'

Hadn't he heard her?

The boy Merlin releases the Dragons
from under King Vortigern's castle

Raine peered down over the side of the saddle. Betelnut tea sloshed around in her stomach and she forgot all about her question

Her stomach had just settled when Little One's wing beats slowed down, and he pulled into one of the openings in the wall. The corridor beyond was lit by glowing crystal chandeliers hanging from the ceiling. Thick carpet covered the floor. Fires burned in golden bowls set into the wall, curling smoke wafted in the air. It was like something out of one of her mum's stories. What would happen if Raine let the book fall open – would it show her a picture of this tunnel with something like: *Raine unknowingly went to her certain doom*, written underneath? Little One stomped down the passageway. He stopped at a floor length curtain and lowered himself, allowing Raine and Little Monkey to scramble down the rope ladder before he stood.

Raine wobbled around to his head on shaky legs. 'Thank you very much for the ride, Little One! And thanks again for saving me!' She kissed him on the cheek.

Little One backed away down the corridor, hiccupping smoke burps.

'I think he likes you!' Monkey laughed.

Raine's cheeks burned as if she'd been sitting in front of a fire.

'Are you ready?'

Raine shook her head. Her stomach flipped around in a dance that made her feel sick. 'No. I don't know where I am, or why I'm here, or even who I am anymore!' She blinked but a tear escaped and trickled down her cheek. She scrubbed it away with her fist.

Monkey scrambled up her trouser leg and hung onto her waist. Raine scooped him up and cuddled him tight.

'Mmmm. Fllmm. Mmmm,' Monkey said.

Raine looked down. She was cuddling him a bit too tight.

'Sorry,' she said, putting him on the ground. 'A cuddle feels nice.'

'For you, maybe. Don't worry. I'm here, and you're about to have all your questions answered. Look at it this way – whatever happens, it can't be worse than before, can it?'

Raine shook her head. No, it couldn't be worse than Bruiser. Anyway, she was having an adventure, and wasn't that what she'd always wanted? She brushed the beautiful material of her outfit. At least here she wasn't stupid, weak Drippy Raine. She ran a hand over her hair, which was already a frizzy mess. She rolled her eyes. Somethings you couldn't change.

'Okay, I'm ready.'

Monkey scampered forward and fished under the curtain. He pulled out a heavy bell-rope and tugged.

'Come!' a deep voice rang out from the other side.

The curtain parted and Monkey pushed her through a doorway. She stumbled into a huge stone room. Raine gaped and spun in a circle. It was like being in a giant jeweller's shop. Gold ornaments glinted against the walls and crystal chandeliers sparkled from the ceiling. Monkey kicked her shin.

'Ow! What's that for?'

Monkey pointed.

A crowd of Western Dragons glared at Raine from stone benches carved into the walls. They weren't whispering or nudging, unlike the creatures in the great hall. She couldn't look at them. Her legs were going to give way. She might throw up. Raine focused on her feet instead. Monkey kicked her again.

'What now? Oh.'

An old dragon marched up to her. Wisps of snowy, white hair sprang out from around its ears. Shaggy eyebrows shadowed deep-set eyes. A yellowed moustache drooped under its horn.

It was dressed in a long, velvet cloak, trimmed with fur. A chunky gold necklace, inlaid with an inscription, hung around its neck. The creature leered at Raine. She did her best to smile back at the dragon, but her mouth twitched, and her legs wobbled like jelly. *Please don't be sick or fall over.*

'Your father's eyes,' the creature muttered in a deep, hoarse voice, 'Different nose, though. Much pointier.' He reached out a sharp, hooked talon. Had her nose offended him? Was he going to rip it off? Raine winced, but he only ruffled her hair.

As his claw connected with her scalp, a force slammed into her body. Her legs buckled. Her mind filled with a rainbow of fireworks. Images flashed. Colours sang. Thunder echoed in her head and fire coursed through her veins. She opened her eyes. Monkey whimpered under her.

'Sorry,' she said, rolling off him.

'What happened?' Raine rubbed her temple and blinked. After-images skipped across the wall, like someone had shone a torch through her eyes and into her brain and had a good rummage around.

'I've never seen the gift so strong in one so

young!' the dragon said to Monkey, hauling Raine to her feet. 'But her magic feels different. There's something strange about it. Perhaps it's because she is completely untrained. That's unfortunate. Morrigan will try and take advantage of it, of course. But still – excellent raw material! You did well to bring her to us, Monkey. You will be rewarded.'

'Bring her? I didn't...' Monkey coughed into his paw. 'Oh, yes, bring her to you! Yes, that was me. Thank you, my Lord!'

'Now, my dear,' the dragon turned to Raine, 'to work!' He banged his cane three times on the stone floor and turned towards the dragons.

'Ladies and Gentlebeasts – I, Lord Smellott of the Underlands, declare this special meeting of the Grand Council open. If any here doubted this child,' he swept his arm back, nearly knocking Raine's head off, 'then let him or her look upon this face! Light runs through her! Can there be any doubt who this child really is?'

Well, actually – yes. Raine frowned. *I have no idea what you're talking about! Who am I? What's going on?* Monkey was completely useless with all his mysterious, "ask no questions; it will all become clear," nonsense. And now, an ancient dragon who should be in a nursing home was messing about, knocking her over, and being rude about her nose. She was sick of being the only one who didn't have a clue what was going on.

'And what do you say, Princess? Will you fulfil the prophecy? Will you save us from the Darkness?'

She shuffled her feet. 'Umm... urgh, I... ah, I'm not sure... I'm not a princess, I'm a kid. I think there's been a mistake,' she mumbled.

A gasp echoed around the room. Lord Smellott's heavy eyebrows shot up his forehead. He stared down at Raine and her toes curled inside her soft boots. A tugging on his robe caught Lord Smellott's attention. Nodding to Monkey, he let the primate scramble up his robes and whisper into his hairy ear. Lord Smellott's eyebrows kept rising until they threatened to disappear into his receding hairline. Monkey scampered back down to the floor and re-joined Raine.

She hissed to Monkey out of the corner of her mouth, 'If someone doesn't tell me what's going on right now, I'm finding a way to go home!'

Frowning and stroking his moustache, the dragon turned to the Grand Council.

'It seems she has been raised an Innocent!' he

boomed. 'She has no idea of her heritage! My brothers and sisters, we have much to discuss!'

The Grand Council whispered behind their claws, their gold neck chains glinting in the flickering light. Lord Smellott turned his attention back to Raine.

'Poor child. How cross you must be with us all! Talking in riddles like this! My apologies. We thought you knew!'

Knew what? I'm sick of this! No one's telling me anything!

Lord Smellott smiled. 'I know how sick of this you must be. No one telling you anything, eh? I bet you're ready to find a way to go home, hmm?'

Wow. Raine blinked. That was exactly what she was thinking! Had he read her mind?

'*Yes,*' replied a gruff voice in her head. '*Sorry, a bit cheeky, I know.*'

Out loud, the aged dragon spoke to Monkey, 'Take your Mistress to the Scrying Well. She will find all her answers there.'

'Yes Lord, thank you, Lord!'

Monkey bowed low. He frowned at Raine and bowed again. She blundered a half curtsy. *At least I didn't fall over.*

'Thank you, Lord Smellott.'

'*I don't hold with formality,*' the voice in her head said, '*You may call me Smelly.*' She swallowed a snigger in time to avoid another kick from Monkey.

***

Raine and Monkey walked back down the corridor. Raine stuck her lower lip out. She dragged her feet along the carpet and trailed behind Monkey.

'You do realise I have absolutely no idea where I am, who I am, or what's happening?' she called after Monkey, who made no signs of turning around, or even slowing. Raine raised her voice. 'Have you got any idea how confusing and *rubbish* all this is? I feel *sick*, and I feel *dizzy!*' She stopped and stamped her foot. She wasn't going one step further. Monkey's shoulders drooped; he turned around and trudged back to Raine.

'Look,' he said. 'I'll tell you what's confusing and *rubbish*. One minute you're a toy monkey in a toyshop, and the next thing you're a sort-of-proper monkey with thoughts and emotions, but no memories. You've got no idea how you got there, but you're stuck in a plastic box, on a shelf, in a toyshop. *That* would make you feel sick and dizzy!'

Crossness and embarrassment crawled around Raine's body. It prickled.

'I'll take you to the Scrying Well because that's what Lord Smellott said to do. The well will show you what happened. You'll be able to see for yourself, okay? And on the way, I'll tell you a bit about where we are. But stop sulking!'

Trying not to look too sulky, Raine nodded, and they carried on walking down the corridor.

'You'd better call Little One. He's down there somewhere,' Monkey said, pointing over the tunnel entrance.

Raine peeked over the edge. Bad mistake. She took a step backwards. Cupping her hands around her mouth, she yelled over the drop.

She turned around to see Monkey sniggering.

'Have you got any idea how far away he is? He'll never hear you!' he said between giggles.

'Well, you're the one who told me to call him!' Raine slumped down on the stone floor. She crossed her arms.

'Well, yes. But properly, you know, with your *mind*.'

Raine rested her aching head against the cool stone wall.

'Like this...' Monkey closed his eyes. A voice like roaring wind swept through Raine's mind. She held onto her head, ears ringing.

'What?' she croaked.

'Go on. Try!' urged Monkey, sitting next to her. 'Everyone here can do it, come on. Shout, inside your head. Like you're shouting at Bruiser!'

It would be unreal to stand up to Bruiser and yell at him. Like it had felt when she bit him. Had she really done that? He was going to kill her when she got home. It wasn't fair. Years of anger bubbled inside. Scrunching her eyes up, she curled her hands into fists. She pictured Bruiser standing in front of her in his sweaty vest and his greasy jeans. Raine pulled her anger up, all the way from her toes through her body. She grabbed every last piece of it and rolled it into a ball. She opened her eyes and roared until her throat hurt. She hurled the ball at Bruiser's head.

Monkey blasted through the air and crashed into the wall. The fires in the braziers sputtered and blew out. He slid to the ground. Monkey lay on his back, cradling his head in his arms and whimpering. Warmth trickled down the side of Raine's face. She wiped it away and looked at her hand. Red.

Thumping footsteps stormed down the corridor.

The Grand Council hurtled towards her, robes flying and swords drawn. The dragons in front skidded to a stop at Raine's feet. The dragons behind barrelled into them, sending Westerns flying like skittles.

The dragons scrambled out of the way. Lord Smellott stalked towards her. He glared down at Raine from under his fierce eyebrows.

'And what's the meaning of all this, young lady?'

'Umm, I was trying to call Little One. Umm, in my head. But all I did was make my ears bleed!' Raine held out her hand. 'See?'

Lord Smellott glared at her. 'I fear that's not all you may have done, child. I'll take you to the Scrying Well myself. There will be less time than we thought!' He turned to the other dragons and ordered, 'Prepare for arms! The call has been sent! The Prophecy is nigh!'

He dropped to all fours. 'Quickly, child, on my back! There's not much time to lose!' Raine scrambled up, gripping his neck chain. Lord Smellott tossed his head at Monkey. 'You too, primate. I hold you entirely responsible for this! What were you thinking? If the Dark One hadn't already realised the Princess is here, she certainly knows now!'

***

A tall figure wrapped in a dark cloak crouched in a cave by the edge of a shadowy forest. A low muttering came from their lips. The small, underground pool the figure crouched beside lit up as something like lightning flashed deep in the water. A mighty roar echoed around the cave. They waved their arm over the pool. The surface cleared. The figure stared into their own dark eyes while the echo died. When the cave was quiet, they stood, turned and stepped off the rock. They made their way around the edge of the pool to the cave entrance, and stood gazing out over their kingdom.

The cave was set in a hillside, and the figure looked down over the forest. The sun was high in the sky, but its brightness did nothing to chase the gloom away. Black, winged shapes skittered around the figure's head. In the distance, beyond the forest, a smooth mountain glimmered like glass.

A second shape padded on all fours from the cave. The cloaked form reached down and stroked the creature's glossy white fur behind its ears. Its broad muzzle opened and a pink tongue rolled out over a row of razor-sharp teeth. A thick tail beat against the stones.

'So, she has come. Fool. All she needed was a little helping hand!' The figure laughed, their fingers tightened in the huge animal's fur, making it whimper. 'It is time to end this dynasty, and the Underlands shall finally be mine!' The animal thumped its tail. 'Prepare the call to arms, Lykoi! The Prophecy is nigh!'

The animal stood up on its hind legs. It rose to its full height, towering over the figure standing next to it. Raising its head towards the sky, it opened its mouth. Its howl was heard throughout the forest below. Cries answered from all over the forest. The flying shapes that had been swooping and diving around the hooded figure turned as one. In a thick column, they flapped away towards the forest. They disappeared, screeching into the darkness. The great dog-like creature dropped back down to all fours. It jumped from the rocky ledge in front of the cave, bounding down the mountain. The cloaked figure grinned and turned back towards the cave.

CHAPTER 5
FAMILY TIES

They left the rest of the Grand Council and flew upwards out of the bustling Hive. They flew past dragon blacksmiths and armourers battering sheets of metal into suits of iron and chain mail. The clang of metal on metal filled Raine's ears. They passed swordsmiths plunging newly hammered swords and spears into cold water, wrapping her in clouds of steam. Raine peered down to the lower floors of the Hive, where massive fires glowed. Flo and her friends threw bunches of herbs into bubbling cauldrons. Raine's empty stomach growled as the smell, like a Sunday roast with all the trimmings, wafted around her. Ranks of warriors trained in the great hall.

They exploded out of the Hive into dazzling

sunlight. Her hands gripped the gold chain, and her knees squeezed either side of Lord Smellott's wide neck. Monkey clung to her waist with his eyes screwed shut. He was as green as a brown monkey can look.

It was a world away from Mum and Scutter's Alley. Lord Smellott hovered at the mouth of the Hive, which was bare rock until halfway down where a line of windswept, stunted trees grew. Below these trees, the mountainside was carpeted in grass, merging with a sunlit forest at its base.

'Actually,' Lord Smellott called back over his shoulder. 'It's a volcano, not a mountain! Extinct now, of course. My forefathers tunnelled out the inside many generations ago. Scutter's Alley must be your home, eh?' The dragon tilted downwards, like an eagle swooping. He dove down the side of the volcano. Raine leaned back and held on for dear life. She wanted to ask how he'd read her mind so easily, but the wind snatched the words from her mouth.

'*It's not hard,*' his gravelly voice rumbled in her head. '*You can do it too. Talk to me. In your thoughts. Think about how you sent out that call, and then do the exact opposite!*'

Instead of bundling her thought up and throwing

it forward, she gently gathered it up, stroked it like a kitten and let it jump out of her mind.

'*So, can you all do this?*' she asked the dragon, projecting the question to him.

'*Excellent! You're a natural, and a quick learner too! I knew you would be! Such a shame you've had no training!*' he replied.

Raine gathered up another thought and pushed it to the front of her mind. '*Yes, but you're still not answering any of my questions, Smelly!*'

'*Anyone who has drunk the waters of the Scrying Well can thought-share. When we're young, all creatures of light are blessed in the waters.*'

'*Did I drink the water in that tea Flo gave me?*' Raine projected. They finished their speedy descent down the side of the mountain and soared over the forest. She eased her tight grip. Her bag, tucked into her tunic for safe keeping, was warm against her chest. It smelt a bit too. Or perhaps that was Lord Smellott, there was a definite whiff of rotten eggs. Monkey still clung to her waist, his eyes shut and muttering under his breath.

'*No,*' Lord Smellott replied in her mind. '*Many years ago, only the Royal family had the gift. All positions of power were held by someone of the bloodline. Then, the*

Royal family was wiped out. The last of the family was the High Priest of the Underlands, and he was attacked near the well. He was found by a young dragon out looking for betelnuts.' His voice paused, and an image of a clearing in a wood flashed into Raine's mind.

Sunlight dappled the grass. Shadows twisted and turned as if the light and the dark were wrestling. In the centre of the clearing, a circle of stones was piled up, several layers deep. A man bent over the stones, his hands plunged into water. He gazed into the centre of the well. His long, blue robe was covered in silver symbols. A gold chain, like the one Raine clutched, hung around his neck. Blind to the shadows squirming at his feet, the man stared into the well. A figure wrapped in a cloak, its face hidden by the hood, stole out of the trees. An enormous snow white wolf loped by its side. The figure crept up behind the man. It raised its hands with a shriek of laughter. Red flames erupted from a wand held in its fingertips.

Raine gripped the chain tighter. Was this the Dark One?

The man slumped down over the well. His body shook.

Raine's palms sweated against the gold chain.

The cloaked figure dropped the wand and danced back into the trees with the wolf capering at its heels.

Moments later, something buzzed into the clearing, darting in and out of the trees. A dragon, not much bigger than Little Thirty-Five. A basket dangled between its front legs and it flew in zigzags, humming to itself. It noticed the man slumped over the well, dropped its basket and flew over. It landed on the man's back, digging its claws into the blue cloak. It shook the man, then started to headbutt him. The dragon snagged its talons deeper into the man's robe and rose into the air. It flapped its wings and heaved backwards. Nothing happened. The dragon flew up to the man's face and peered at him.

The small dragon fluttered around, flitting between the injured man and the trees, as if unsure whether to stay or go and get help.

'Who's there?' the man croaked.

The dragon stood on the edge of the well. 'It's me, High Priest. Young Smelly. You're at the well. You're hurt! Just lie here, and I'll go and get some help!'

Raine gasped. She was watching a young Lord Smellott. It must be a memory of his, but why was he giving her an ancient history lesson now?

The man whispered, 'No, there's nothing you can

do. The witch has filled me with dark energy. I feel it fighting the light within me, turning me to stone.'

The man's face and the fingers trailing in the well were turning grey. 'Cut me on my palm, Smelly. I have seen the future in the well. I need to share it. There are dark days ahead for the Underlands, but one of pure-blood and human-blood will come to us from Skywards. There will be a battle between light and dark. The future of all the worlds will lie in the balance,' his voice grew weaker. 'Cut me. My blood will give the waters the gift of sight. You will see what I see.'

The dragon stood with his head bowed. He rose and slashed the man's hand with his taloned feet. The dragon jumped down into the well. He burst out a few seconds later and shook pink water droplets from his hide. Smellott grew. His limbs extended; his wings rose from his back. He changed from his cat-like size to the giant Raine rode on. His features grew sharper, and his eyebrows sprouted out shaggy hairs. Smellott picked up the wand lying on the ground. Holding it high above his head, he roared and flung the wand into the well.

The picture cleared from Raine's mind. Who had killed the High Priest, and what did it have to do with her?

CHAPTER 6
A SCRYING SHAME

Lord Smellott circled lower and with a shared thought to, '*Hang on!*' he dove into the forest. They came to a skidding stop at the edge of a grass clearing circled by tall, dark leafed trees. Sunlight filtered through and tapped Raine's face like warm fingertips. Monkey scrambled off the dragon's back and, one paw clamped over his mouth, ran for the nearest tree.

'Sorry,' he groaned behind his paw, 'not a very good air traveller. Unlucky for a wizard's familiar, really. Never could get the hang of flying carpets.'

Lord Smellott and Raine faced each other.

'So, you were the one who found him? Who was he? And what happened to you? What's Underland?

And Skyworld?' Raine demanded, frowning.

'The Underlands and Skywards,' Lord Smellott corrected, 'are our two worlds, Raine. Separated by the thinnest of walls.'

The wall in her basement, which had broken apart in her hands. She'd been right about something at least; it wasn't a proper wall at all.

'Of course,' he continued, 'there are many worlds, but not all so close and connected as ours. The Underlands is a world of dark and light, good and bad, much like your own. But unlike you humans, with your free will to choose dark or light – good or evil – we're born to one side and don't change unless someone with stronger magic changes us. But that is almost unheard of and incredibly dangerous. I've only ever seen it happen once.'

'What do you mean stronger magic? Why am I here?'

'We're all lower magic creatures here now, Raine. We can read minds, perform a few tricks. And like I said, we're born either light or dark. Magic itself usually keeps a balance between the numbers. But a Dark One came to the Underlands ten years ago. She changed a creature of light with higher magic, and pulled him into the darkness. She upset the balance.

The darkness has been spreading ever since. Now she has enough power, and enough followers, to take over the Underlands.'

He looked into Raine's eyes. She squared her shoulders and lifted her chin but, judging by his sigh, she didn't do a very good job. 'You're our only hope, Raine. We need your higher magic. You're the only one left who can stop this.'

'Am I the pure-blood the man at the well spoke about? Was my mum Queen? Is that what this is all about? And what happened to you, Smelly?'

The dragon burped two long plumes of smoke into Raine's hair. 'Yes, my child, you're of royal blood, and this battle is all you have as a legacy. But it's not from your mother. She's an ordinary human.'

Monkey snorted. 'Sorry, I think I swallowed a fly.' He walked away, muttering to himself.

'The man at the well was Lord Duro. Your father's cousin—'

'My father?' Raine grabbed the front of Lord Smellott's cloak. 'Is he here? Who is he? Can I see him?'

Lord Smellott bent down until they were eye to eye. 'Lord Duro was the High Priest of the Source of Light, and the last of the Royal line, child...'

'You m – mean, my f – father?'

Lord Smellott shifted from foot to foot. He eventually nodded.

To find her father and then have him taken away, it wasn't fair! She hid her face in her hands. Monkey clutched her leg, but it did nothing to comfort her. For the first time in her life, no story would be able to keep her father alive. Every single night as she lay in bed, listening to Bruiser shouting, she'd imagined the different ways she'd go and find her dad, and the adventures they'd have. How could it end like this? She'd been so sure they'd be back together one day.

'Wha... What... ha... ha... happened to him?'

Lord Smellott stepped back, exposing the well she had seen in her mind. A stone statue lay half in the well, its cheek resting on the edge and its hands in the water. The priest. He was still there. Raine walked over and peered over the edge.

'So, if I drink this, I'll know what happened? Like you did? Won't it make me old, too?' she asked.

'You're of royal blood. You possess higher magic, which means you already have the sight. Look within the well, and you will see. But no, to drink wouldn't make you old. I had to give up my childhood to lead the other creatures of light. We had to find a new way of living with the Royal Family gone. Who would have listened to a child? That was Lord Duro's last gift to us. I'm lucky. We dragons live for hundreds of years. I only sacrificed a small part of my life.'

The dragon patted Raine's shoulder, almost pushing her into the well, and motioned for Monkey to follow him. Raine turned back to the dark depths of the water and saw shapes writhing down there.

At the edge of the clearing Lord Smellott called out, 'Look into the waters and ask for the truth! The Source of Light will guide you.'

Raine watched the water brighten as if fireworks exploded under the surface. The colours swirled and joined together.

***

A little later, Raine and Monkey sat side by side next to the glowing embers of a campfire. Next to them lay some red berries and small, blue mushrooms Lord Smellott and Monkey had foraged while Raine was at the Scrying Well. Night had fallen, and the forest was quiet. Lord Smellott stalked around the edge of the clearing muttering under his breath and sprinkling well-water on the ground. He had explained to Raine that the forest was too dangerous to travel at night. They would set off at first light. In the meantime, his protection spell and the pure water of the well would keep them safe as they slept. Raine tossed blades of grass into the remains of the fire. They curled and charred.

'Are you okay?' Monkey asked.

Raine shrugged and chucked a twig on the fire. It should have been weird to be sitting talking to him, but it was the least of her worries.

'I'm not sure. I don't know if I understand everything I saw in the water.'

'Well, why don't you tell it to me? Like a story?'

'I don't think I can. I saw pictures – different people; a baby, some old lady, two men in crowns and, I think Mum, except she looked young. And happy...' It was no good, everything was a jumble. Her shoulders slumped and she scratched a sad face in the dirt with the stick she'd been chewing. 'Anyway, what's the point? I thought telling stories about my dad would keep him alive, but it didn't. He's dead.'

'He's not!' The voice was muffled and squeaky.

Raine stopped scratching in the dirt. 'Did you hear that?'

Monkey spoke around a mouthful of berries, 'What?'

'Nothing. I thought I heard something. I'm tired, I guess. Anyway, there's no point telling stories – they're not real.'

'They are!' There was that voice again. Not funny. She glared at Monkey.

'Monkey, stop messing around. I already told you, I'm tired. I can't be bothered with you mucking about.'

Monkey swallowed an enormous mouthful of mushrooms. His eyes bulged. 'What are you talking about?' Bits of mushroom sprayed the ground as he spoke. 'By the way, where's your bag going?'

What was Monkey talking about? Her bag was sitting on the grass near her leg, where she'd left it. Monkey must have pushed it while they were talking though because she couldn't reach it. Raine's jaw clenched, and her teeth ground together. 'Stop it, okay? You're not funny! It's just a stupid bag!'

Raine kicked out and sent the bag skidding across the ground.

'Ow!' the bag said, in a squeaky, muffled voice. A tendril of smelly smoke curled out from under the buckle. 'That hurt,' the bag whimpered. The bag puffed out as if it was breathing, and a small green and yellow shape crawled out from the opening in a cloud of grey smoke.

'Little Thirty-Five!' Raine ran over and gathered the little dragon up, 'I'm so sorry! I didn't know you were in there! Are you alright?' She looked around, Smelly was on the other side of the clearing, engrossed in his protection spells. 'What are you doing here?' Raine hissed, 'Flo'll kill you. And me.'

'I'm going to help you. On your Quest.'

'But it'll be dangerous, and you're a baby.' His needle claws dug into her palm. Raine winced.

Little Thirty-Five puffed out his chest and stood as tall as he could.

'I'm not *a* baby. I'm *Mum's* baby and she'll never let me grow up, and never let me have an adventure, and never be like Little One. Anyway, I know the story, and don't you want to hear it?'

She did want to know the story, Little Thirty-Five was right. Life would have been completely different if she'd had her dad around. She needed to know what had happened to him. But hadn't he said her dad wasn't dead when he was hiding in the bag? The bag that had been suspiciously hot and smelly since they left the Grand Council. He was quite brave for such a little thing. Braver than her.

Raine went back to Monkey, shielding Little Thirty-Five in her hand so Smelly wouldn't see, and sat down.

Monkey nodded at the small dragon. 'You made it, then.'

'You knew he was in there?' Raine said, 'And you didn't tell me?'

'No, not knew. Guessed. He's ready for an adventure, or he wouldn't have made it into your cellar in the first place. Sounds a bit like someone else.' Monkey smirked. She wasn't going to give him the satisfaction of admitting he was right.

'Well, how do you know the story? Smelly told me to come and find out at the well, but I can't understand any of it.'

Little Thirty-Five sat down on Raine's palm, with his tail wrapped around his legs and his wings neatly folded over his back. He burped and the smoke went straight up Raine's nose, again. It was like she had a smoke magnet up there.

'Those two men you saw? That was the twin princes. Mum was their nurse when they were babies. She never shuts up about them. She's told me the story a million times, at least.'

'Was one of them my dad? I don't even know what he looks like. Mum said Bruiser threw all our photos away. She never talks about him, and I don't remember him.'

Little Thirty-Five nodded. 'Once upon a time there were twin brothers – The Princes of Light; Clarus and Bardus. They ruled the Underlands together in perfect balance and harmony. One day they went out unicorn riding—'

'Woah, unicorns aren't real. That's a fairytale,' Raine interrupted. Monkey rolled his eyes, tutted and handed her the book.

'Oh.' The book fell open on another picture page. Raine clapped it shut. 'I'll believe everything from now on, I think. Hang on, are there still unicorns here? In this wood?'

'No. The witch has killed them all. Taken their magic.'

Raine's stomach lurched. What kind of person would kill a unicorn?

Little Thirty-Five burped and continued, 'Somehow, they ended up in Skywards, and Prince Clarus met a beautiful lady. They fell in love, and the prince went to live there because he couldn't bring a human back with him.'

'Why not?' Raine massaged her head. It didn't help. Her brain was going to explode.

Little Thirty-Five shrugged. 'Mum never said. She said he went to live there, and they had a baby. A girl. Then Prince Bardus became King and ruled the Underlands all by himself. Until he met a lady as well, when he was hunting a chimera in the Dark Forest that had been catching creatures of light—'

'A what?' Raine interrupted. *Unimagined Lands and True Tales* started to grow warm in her hand. Raine held it out and let the pages fall open. She had to admit, having a magical guidebook was pretty cool, even if the warm cover did feel like skin. But it was best not to think about that. Sure enough, the pages rested at a picture of a creature with a lion's head, a goat's body and a snake for a tail.

'Anyway, he didn't find the chimera but he did find a beautiful woman lost in the forest and she had ambrosia—'

'Ambrosia? Isn't that a kind of fruit salad? She was walking around, lost in a forest with a bowl of dessert?' Raine was beginning to believe there were many things in this world that didn't make sense, but running around a spooky wood waving dessert about was pushing it.

The Chimera is a female, fire breathing
monster with the strength of a lion, the
cunning of a goat and a snake's venom.
It can only be killed with molten lead.

Little Thirty-Five shook his head. 'No, that thing where you can't remember anything. What's it called?'

Raine shrugged. 'Dunno. Can't remember. Magnesia?'

'That's not right.'

Monkey joined in, 'Indonesia?'

'Doesn't matter. She didn't know her name or how she got to the forest or anything, so King Bardus took her home with him. And they fell in love. And then they had a baby boy. But one day,' Little Thirty-Five deepened his voice into a theatrical squeak, 'Tragedy struck.' The effort caused a little tongue of flame to shoot out from his bottom and smoulder on the grass. Raine stomped it out before they set the forest on fire. She snuck a glance at Smelly. Luckily, he was facing away on the other side of the clearing. 'One day, his wife and son went for a walk in the forest, but they never came back. All that was found of them were some blood-stained clothes. The king went crazy with grief. He spent more and more time in the Dark Forest, and one day he met the wicked witch there.'

Raine's shoulders slumped. *Bet that witch has got something to do with this Prophecy thing.*

'She convinced him that his twin brother had murdered his wife and son. So they joined forces and lured the brother to the Crystal Mountain. The story says they killed him there and threw his body in the mountain, but my mum says—'

'That's what the pictures in the well were,' Raine whispered. She hung her head. 'I think I know the rest of the story anyway. Prince Clarus was my dad, wasn't he? And the lady is my mum, and I'm the baby girl.'

Black spots flickered at the edges of her eyes. Her pulse thundered in her ears like crashing waves. Her head pounded. Her muscles tensed. She sprang to her feet. 'This witch and King Whatever killed my dad and ruined my mum's life!' She smashed her fist into the palm of her hand. 'Now I'm going to kill them too!'

Raine sprinted to the well. She bent over the edge, next to the statue, and held her hand out. She threw her thoughts down into the water. Anger sent her mind storming down to the bottom of the well. She found what she was looking for. A black wand came hurtling up from the depths of the well and landed with a loud smack in Raine's outstretched hand. She smirked and turned to Monkey.

'Rather fitting, don't you think?' she asked. She bounced up and down on the balls of her feet. Wild energy raced through her. 'I'll use the wand they used! I'll kill that witch and the prince!'

Lord Smellott thundered over. He snatched the wand out of Raine's hand. 'That's not you talking, girl! That's the wand!' He held it above Raine's head out of reach. She danced about, trying to grab it. 'This wand is evil! Made with the fires of darkness! It's tasted destruction, and it wants to taste it again!' Smelly said.

Raine hissed and jumped. She missed the wand and landed on the statue. 'Ow!' She rubbed her banged elbow. Raine's blood stopped boiling in her veins. Her heartbeat slowed. She sat on the statue, panting. Her hands trembled. 'How did I get *that,*' she stood up and pointed at the wand with a shaky finger, 'out of the well? I didn't know I could do stuff like that!'

'No, but the wand did,' Lord Smellott said, holding it away like a dirty sock. 'It called to you. That's the trouble with you humans, you're too easy to tempt. Always changing from one side to the next.'

'But I'm a creature of light!'

'You're a halfling, my dear. Half-daughter of light

and half-human. It will either be your downfall, or it will save you. Only time will tell. But it's up to you to be aware, to control the temptation. Or Morrigan will control you – and then I fear both worlds are doomed!'

Monkey flinched and made a gesture in the air with his paw before tapping his forehead three times.

Raine frowned. *What now?* 'What on earth are you doing?'

'Warding off the Evil One – She Who Sees All.'

Raine lifted an eyebrow. 'Oh yes, I see. Of course you are.'

'The Sorceress Morrigan, Creature of Darkness, Queen of Chaos.'

'The one who killed my father? I'll give *her* chaos!' Raine snarled.

Lord Smellott held up a claw. 'How can you fight chaos with chaos? Hatred with hatred? Darkness with darkness? Your father was a creature of light. Where do you think your strongest powers lie?'

Raine groaned. It was all too complicated. But she was there for a reason. She slumped down next to the statue.

I'm here to rebalance the Underlands. The idea

whispered to her. Underneath all her anger, there was something else. She concentrated. Something peaceful. Like a deep, still pool. Gradually, the calm waters put out the flames of her anger. To fight Morrigan, she had to harness the power of light.

She imagined diving into the pool of calmness, its soothing waters closing over her head. She floated in peaceful stillness. She focused on all these feelings and pointed at the wand dangling from Lord Smellott's grip. It burst into bright blue flame. The dragon dropped it with a yelp. The trio stood around the wand, watching it burn on the ground. The fire flickered and went out. A white feather lay on the grass in its place.

Smellott bent down. 'Back in the well with you!'

'No!' Raine grabbed the feather. 'I'll need it.' How did she know that?

'Very well but be careful.' Smellott looked at Little Thirty-Five, who had perched on Raine's shoulder like a tiny parrot. 'And as for you, what do you think you're doing here? You will return to the Hive immediately.'

'No!' Little Thirty-Five yelled in his loudest cheep, right in Raine's ear – which at least meant the cloud of toxic smoke went in her ear, instead of up her nose. 'I'm going with them! She needs me! I know all about the prince and the witch, I can help her!'

Lord Smellott frowned from under his huge eyebrows. 'I see a younger me in you, my lad. But no, you must return with me – your mother will be worried.'

'I wrote her a note. She knows the princess will look after me.'

'Your mother will kill me.'

'No, she won't. She likes you. Like, *like* likes you – I heard her telling Aunty Doris.'

Raine, Monkey and Little Thirty-Five sniggered as the green left Lord Smellott's face to be replaced with a rosy pink. He smiled at the ground before growling at them all, 'It's late! We must rest before the morrow.' He stalked away.

Raine yawned and rubbed her eyes. Doing magic wasn't as easy as it looked. They settled down for the night. They lay down next to the remains of the fire, all four snuggled up under Lord Smellott's cloak. Monkey was curled up against Raine's back, Little Thirty-Five snored and burped next to her head. She'd never get to sleep. Shrieks echoed in the distance. If only she could block her ears. She yawned. Monkey was warm against her. She yawned again.

CHAPTER 6
DESTINY CALLS

The sun was rising over the treetops when they broke camp the next morning. The chill of the night still clung to the air, and they moved like wooden puppets about the clearing. They had breakfasted on well-water and plants boiled over the campfire, sweetened with more berries Monkey found high up in the treetops. Scampering down from these same treetops he now reported to Lord Smellott that the forest seemed quiet, and he could see no movement out of the ordinary.

Lord Smellott drew Raine to him and walked her towards the well.

'The spells have kept our presence here unknown overnight, and the creatures of darkness won't come near the well, so for the moment, we're safe. But, once you have left the protection of this place, it won't take Morrigan long to find you.' He looked into Raine's eyes. 'Remember to keep your light close and don't let her goad you into darkness. There's something different about your magic. I don't know why, but it's not the same as the rest of your bloodline.'

'What about King Bardus?' Raine said, 'Will he come here too? Do I need to fight him?'

The dragon shook his head. 'He disappeared straight after killing his brother. We think the witch killed him after she had no use for him.'

Little Thirty-Five flapped up, 'Mum says—'

'Sshh,' Lord Smellott scolded. 'He wasn't the one with power, my dear. Like the rest of us, he was a pawn in her game. The prophecy tells us – hang on.' He scrabbled about inside his cloak. 'I must have left it behind. I'll see if I can remember it all.'

Raine's leg was getting warm again. The book must have something to show her. She reached into her bag and grabbed the feather and the book. As usual, it opened where she needed to read.

'That's it? That's the prophecy? It's not much of an instruction manual, is it? Doesn't really *help me* much.'

When our worlds are rent apart
and Darkness stalks the Light,
from up above returns our daughter
to give us back our right.
Her half-blood line may save us yet,
in the last stage of our fight.
She will battle evil with good
and face the Witch of the Night.

If she should fail and Darkness wins,
two worlds they will be lost.
Ruled by the Queen of Chaos
and Light will be the cost.
All will live in violent misery,
the world to be damned.
Creatures of the Light rise up
and fight to save our land.

Lord Smellott shuffled his feet in the grass. 'Well,' he mumbled at the ground, 'I didn't have a lot of time, and umm... I'm not much of a poet, but... umm... I think it gets the point across, doesn't it?'

'Yes. I think it does. If I don't win this fight and kill this Witch of the Night, your world and my world will be ruled by her forever. That's not a good thing, is it?'

'Exactly. And now you must go. Monkey and Little Thirty-Five will take you to where you'll find her. But beware, she may find you first.' He shook his head and held up a curled talon. 'Try to keep your thoughts inside your head. She'll be looking for you, and she'll use your thoughts to track you. Your magic will draw her to you. She'll want your power; it will make her even stronger.'

'Aren't you coming with us?' Raine's eyes stung. She wouldn't cry. She wouldn't.

'I must return to the Hive. We are *all* at war. Morrigan is backed by her creatures of darkness. You, Daughter of Light, have all of us behind you. I'll see you again, Raine, but this is your battle, and I can't travel with you. It's your destiny, and you're the only one left with the power to stop the sorceress, Morrigan. And then the Underlands will be yours to rule.'

How was a kid meant to stop a sorceress? Or rule a whole world, even if she wanted to? She couldn't even stop people calling her Drippy Raine.

'We must hurry,' Lord Smellott said. 'She'll be her strongest at nightfall; you must find her before then. Search the well and see if you can see what she's doing.'

Raine stretched over the water and gazed into its depths. How was she supposed to conjure an image of a wicked witch she'd never even seen? She probed the water with her mind, like sticking a finger in a drink. A hooded figure appeared in the water. It melted into the face of a pretty, dark-haired young woman. She was waving and laughing and holding up a baby in her arms. Her image was replaced by another, the heavily bearded face of a man with wild, grey hair and sad, brown eyes. His lips moved, but as hard as Raine tried, she couldn't hear what he was saying. His features shifted and she stared into the cold, flat eyes of Bruiser. She recoiled. Why would the well show her his face? What did he have to do with any of this?

She swallowed. The lump in her throat stayed where it was. 'I couldn't see her. All I saw was a young woman and a baby. She looked a bit like Mum. And I saw an old man. Then I saw my stepfather, but he's just a stupid bully – he's got nothing to do with any of this.'

'It will become clear to you, Raine. The well only shows the truth.'

Raine rested a hand against the stone figure next to her. A bolt of icy lightning so cold it burned, flashed through her. Her nerves jangled and her skin stung. She snatched her hand away. 'He's not dead! I can feel him! I can feel his light!'

'What? But I saw him turn to stone!' Smellott said.

'I promise! I can feel him in there!' Raine put her hand on the stone figure's cheek. Her fingers froze. A cold, calming power coursed from the statue. It seeped from her hand, up her arm and spread through her body.

She stood up straight and took a deep breath. 'I'm ready.'

The dragon bowed. With a flap of his immense wings he was gone, rising over the treetops, and heading towards the Hive.

Raine sank to the ground, cradling her head in her hands. 'What on earth am I going to do? I don't know how to fight! I haven't even got a weapon! And Smelly's gone too!'

Monkey scampered over and tapped her on the knee. 'I don't think it matters. I don't think you need a weapon. I saw the light when you touched that statue. There's more to you than even Smellott knows. But we have to go. And face whatever will be. Come on, we've got a long way to go!'

'I know. It's just that, well, yesterday I was Drippy Raine and today...' She didn't have the words. She shrugged and ran a hand over her messy hair.

'Come on then,' she said. It didn't feel like she had a choice, so she'd better get on with it. 'I suppose you know where we're going?'

'Yes, we umm, need to go to the, err, the... Crystal Mountain,' Monkey said.

'You mean to the place where they killed... where my father...?'

Monkey nodded.

'And I'm not supposed to get angry?' Burning, bubbling anger coursed through her veins like lava. Her heart pounded in her ears. She couldn't hear anything else. It got louder and louder.

'I've got to face th—the... *witch* who killed my father, at the place she murdered him! And I'm supposed to—what? Tell her I love her and cuddle her to death?' Raine started kicking at the trees around her. She thumped them with her fists and tore leaves off their branches.

'Yes, or something like that, I suppose. Not what you're doing now, anyway.' Monkey waited. Raine stopped harassing the innocent trees. She dropped a handful of leaves. Monkey was right. This must be what Smelly meant by free will.

'It makes my blood boil!' she said through gritted teeth. 'Why do I have to be the good one?'

Monkey took Raine's hand. 'Someone has to be. Come on, Raine. It's time to go. It's a now or never sort of thing.' Hand in hand, Little Thirty-Five circling their heads, they left the clearing and picked a path through the dense undergrowth of the surrounding woods.

CHAPTER 8
NOT SO FAIR FAIRIES

It didn't take Monkey long to find the stream he was looking for. They followed its course through the woods towards the Crystal Mountain. The morning was bright and sunny. They walked side by side next to the pretty, clear stream. The water gurgled as it danced over rocks, and dragonflies flitted over the surface of the stream. With the sun beating down on her back, it was easy to forget the task that lay ahead. Raine listened with half an ear to Monkey, trotting along beside her and telling funny stories of his adventures with Uncle Johnny. Raine's mind wandered. How was Mum? Had she realised Raine was missing? She should have left a note behind.

Little Thirty-Five darted ahead, chasing dragonflies and leaving a trail of smoke behind him at Raine's nose height.

As the morning wore on, Monkey disappeared now and then, reappearing with berries and fruit that he gave to Raine. On one occasion when Monkey had been gone a while and Little Thirty-Five was zipping about downstream, Raine sat down. She was tired. It couldn't do any harm to take a break. She chose a flat rock and slipped off her leather boots. She rolled up her trouser legs and dangled her feet into the stream. Sunlight warmed her face.

Raine lay back. The water over the rocks sounded like voices. It was soothing and peaceful. Her muscles relaxed. But, no, that *was* a voice – it must be Monkey, back from his wandering.

Her stomach rumbled. She wouldn't mind something more than berries to eat. The voice whispered near her ear. She opened an eye, but there was no one nearby. Just the dragonflies weaving in and out of the dappled sunlight where the water lapped around her legs.

Dragonflies that were *laughing* as they darted around. Wearing floaty dresses and gauzy little suits. With people faces and hair. So, not dragonflies then, more like... well, fairies. Raine studied them through half-closed eyes. They were no bigger than her thumb. Tiny boys and girls with see-through wings shimmering in the sunlight.

One of them flew up and landed on her nose. She sneezed. A gang of little people crowded around her head. She opened her eyes fully. They fluttered away, hovered in the air and whispered behind their hands.

'Don't worry.' Raine smiled. 'I won't hurt you. I'm your friend.' It was the same words she'd said to Little Thirty-Five back in the basement – but these beautiful fairies couldn't be any more different than her funny-looking, smelly little buddy.

A red-haired boy flew up to her face.

'What are you?'

'Um, well, I'm a human,' Raine said, 'I think.'

The boy looked back to his companions. 'Where are you from? There aren't any humans here!'

'Um, Skywards?'

A shiny black beetle flew upstream towards them. A young woman dressed in shimmering silver rode on its back. Under a tiny flower crown, white-blonde hair trailed behind her. Pulling on the reins, the young woman brought the beetle to a stop on

Raine's rock. She climbed off, curtsied and clicked her fingers at the fairy children. They unloaded tiny jars tied to the beetle's saddle.

'Welcome to the Forest, Human! Will you drink fairy nectar with us, as a sign of our friendship?'

A fairy girl flew up to Raine, cupping an acorn brimming with golden liquid.

Raine hesitated. Should she wait for Monkey to come back? But he'd been gone a long time and she was hungry and thirsty. It was such a tiny amount of nectar, surely it would be fine. And she didn't want to be rude. It sounded like she'd need all the help she could get from these creatures of light that Lord Smellott kept talking about. Although how much help could a bunch of fairy children be?

Raine took the acorn and drained it. Her face screwed up. *Bleurgh!* Surely nectar should be delicious. Her stomach gurgled. A boy with purple wings held another acorn to her lips. Oh well. She held her breath and swallowed. It wasn't one of those drinks that tastes better after the first glass.

She finished her drink and put the acorn on the rock next to her. She stretched her heavy limbs. The fairy children skittered over the stream, playing tag. Now and then, one of them would flutter over towards Raine and study her. It was sweet of them to keep checking on her. But where was Monkey? He'd been gone for ages. And what was Little Thirty-Five doing? She shouldn't have let him wander off. Flo would be furious.

Her head drooped. She was so tired. She'd just lie down for a second and then go to find Little Thirty-Five. The sun slipped behind a cloud and Raine shivered. Her eyelids drooped. Her eyelashes were as heavy as lead. It was like being stuck in a dream she couldn't wake up from.

Where was Monkey? Why was she so tired? She rubbed her arms with her hands. She was freezing. Her skin prickled and her hairs stood on end.

Something wasn't right.

I want my mum. But she might not even see her mum ever again. What if it all went wrong and she lost the war? What if she got all the dragons killed? What if Monkey had been turned back into a toy, and never came back?

Raine's eyes snapped open, and she shot up on the rock. Tears streamed down her face. She bawled; her arms wrapped tightly around herself. She howled and rocked. How could she have been so stupid to agree to this quest? The fairy children gathered close around her – but what could they do to make her feel better? She was going to get them all killed! She wasn't good enough for this quest! She wasn't a princess; she was a stupid kid who didn't know anything! A hot, sick feeling bubbled in her chest. The fist was back, clamped around her heart. She couldn't breathe.

Her fingers scrabbled against the rock, suddenly desperate to leave this place. Her nail snapped, sending a flash of pain through her. Raine cried out. The fairies crept closer. Their gleeful smiles widened. Raine sobbed. Their teeth grew longer and sharper. Their eyes changed from a clear, sky-blue to a deep, glowing red. Raine wailed. Pointed teeth flashed in the sun. The children stretched and swelled. They gathered in a tight group around her. Raine whimpered in the iciness of their shadows.

A small shape darted up the stream surface and ducked under a fairy, who tried to grab it but missed and fell in the stream.

'Look at me, Raine! Not them! Look at me!' Little Thirty-Five whizzed around Raine. The children snatched at the air, but he was too fast for their clumsy fingers.

'It's Scary Fairy! Mum says she eats grumpy little

dragons who won't stop sulking!' Little Thirty-Five hovered in front of Raine's face. 'You've got to cheer up!'

Raine heaved and hiccupped. 'I can't! I'm never going to see Mum again! I'm going to get us all killed!'

The fairies closed in tighter around her.

The beetle riding fairy swooped to grab Little Thirty-Five. He shot into the air. She overbalanced and fell head-first into the stream.

Raine giggled.

The children stopped moving towards her.

The fairy sat up, her muddy hair hung down over her face. A frog sat on her head.

Raine sniggered.

The fairies backed away.

Little Thirty-Five landed on Raine's rock. He was panting. He pointed at the fairy in the river, who was trying to flap her soaking wings. 'That's Scary Fairy. You've got to be happy. They're allergic to it.'

Scary Fairy scowled. The frog ribbited.

Raine and Little Thirty-Five cackled. The fairies shrank.

'I think I've got an idea!' Raine reached into her bag and pulled out the feather. She tickled Little Thirty-Five under his wing. He yelped and squealed. She tickled him again, under his chin. He giggled and hiccupped. A flame shot out of his bottom and set a fairy's wings on fire. The fairy jumped into the stream and knocked Scary Fairy under the water again.

Raine snorted. Which made them both laugh harder.

The fairies shrivelled.

Raine tickled Little Thirty-Five, who zoomed around aiming fart fire at the fairies.

They writhed and squirmed, shrinking smaller and smaller. With a little plink, like a single piano note, the whole group vanished.

Slow clapping boomed from the riverbank. Raine slumped on her rock. Little Thirty-Five landed on her head.

'Have you been there the whole time?' she asked Monkey.

He skipped over to her rock and sat down.

'Not the whole time. Did they give you something to drink? I bet they did! They fed you dark energy, Raine!'

'Is that why I felt so sad?'

Monkey nodded. 'It was a trick. What were you thinking about?'

'Mum, mostly. She must be worried. She might think I'm dead!' Raine's lip wobbled. It might have all been a fairy trick, but she was still worried about her mum.

Monkey's warm paw gripped her shoulder. 'Why don't you check?'

'How? I can't exactly ring her, can I?' Raine held her hand like an imaginary phone up to her ear, '"Oh, hi Mum, I'm in a different world with a talking monkey and a dragon but I'll be back for tea if a witch doesn't kill me first. Bye!"'

Monkey grabbed Raine's hand and put the feather in it.

'Actually, you can. Sort of. It's more of a video call. On mute.'

Raine stroked the feather. 'A feather? Are you feeling alright, Monkey?'

He sighed. 'It's not really a feather, is it? It's *really* a wand, but you did something funny to it. So why don't you wave it about and see what happens?'

That didn't seem like a very sensible idea.

Too much could go wrong if she was stupid enough to do what Monkey said. The last time she'd done what he suggested and tried to call Little One, she'd nearly ruined everything by yelling at Bruiser. Raine held her breath and waggled the feather up and down.

Her ears crackled, her eyes smarted, and her legs wobbled. Electricity crackled up and down her body. Raine shut her eyes and looked into the darkness. A picture formed. Her mum was in the basement with a torch tucked under her chin. She kneeled on the floor and took a penknife from her apron pocket. Wedging it between two floorboards, she used the blade to lever up one of the boards. Elsie took a thin, straight, white stick from under the floor and shoved it down the front of her dress. She dragged the mangy looking old rug from where it was propped against the wall. Hadn't Raine left it in a heap on the floor? When her mum lay both hands on the carpet, it flashed a golden colour. So Raine hadn't imagined it. Then she stood up and looked straight at Raine. She smiled and tapped her nose.

***

It was deepest, darkest midnight in Scutter's Alley. Bursts of moonlight shone through clouds pushed along by an angry wind. A slender figure slipped out of Number Twenty-Six, pulling the door closed behind her. There wasn't much chance of Bruiser waking up after the sleeping draught she'd slipped into his soup. But to make sure, she'd given his head a good whack with her broomstick too. A tiny smile tugged up the corner of Elsie's mouth. She'd been dying to give that brute a taste of his own medicine for years, but as a Guardian she had to obey the Lore. Now she was going help her daughter, Raine, and keep Bruiser out of the picture any way she could. To be honest, the second whack and muttering, 'This one's for Raine, scumbag!' might have been pushing it a bit.

Elsie crept down the alley, sticking to the shadows, dragging a long shape behind her. Her witch's nose twitched. Dark energy. It was the same smell that had led her to the basement. She had slipped a few special herbs in the pot of soup, and once Bruiser was slurping away, she had followed her nose. A snap of her fingers had cast enough light to see that Raine had gone.

The Gateway Elsie had been guarding had knit itself shut since Raine and Monkey kicked their way through. Elsie sniffed. It didn't matter how innocent the gateway had tried to look, pretending to be a wall again. The basement stank of magic. Big magic. The kind of magic only practised by the most experienced of witches and wizards. Or the baddest, who don't use it carefully at all and end up in all sorts of trouble. Elsie knew exactly who had been messing about with the Gateway. *Morrigan.*

A tall, broad figure stepped out of the shadows. Elsie jumped, her heart thumping. The big man bowed low and touched his finger to Elsie's outstretched hand. A blue spark flashed between them.

'You called, Great One?' The Magnificent Johnny towered over Elsie in his pointed hat. The silver stars on his robes shone in the moonlight.

Elsie was tiny and drab next to him in her brown coat and slippers. 'Oh, don't call me that! Not after everything we've been through! You were my teacher, for goodness' sake!'

Johnny's cheeks glowed as red as his robes. Powerful wizards aren't used to getting told-off.

Elsie reached out and grabbed his hand. He winced. Her elegant, bony fingers squashed his own sausages into a sweaty ball. 'It doesn't matter, Johnny! None of it! She's gone!' A tear dripped from the end of a nose as long and bony as her fingers. 'She's gone through. I can *smell* it!

Johnny paled. His chins wobbled. He looked at the ground and stamped his curly-toed shoe. 'Down there? But she's not ready!'

'I know that! Do you think I don't know that? And all she's got is that blasted monkey! How's he going to keep her safe?'

'Now then,' Johnny tried to calm Elsie down. When witches get cross, bad things happen. 'Monkey's loyal. He'll do his best. You know he will.'

Elsie's claw-like grip loosened. 'But he's only a monkey. He's not even a real monkey. I never did understand why I couldn't have a cat, like all the other girls.'

Johnny couldn't help himself. The words popped out, 'Morrigan had a wolf.'

Stony silence.

'Well, how did Raine get down there?' he asked.

'Bardus put her in the cellar.'

'Ah. Does he know about the Gateway?'

Elsie shook her head. 'I couldn't risk him finding it and going back. I've been feeding him henbane tea for years.'

'To make him forget?'

'That's why he's so angry all the time, it's one of

the side effects. But I can't use magic, can I?

'And?'

'And I just hit him with my broom. But it's not magic if I'm not flying on it. It doesn't count.'

'So, it was Morrigan?'

'Yes. The cellar stinks of magic. I think Raine's Glimmer got too strong and weakened the Gateway. She was too close to it. Morrigan is powerful enough to open it from the other side if there was a crack in it.'

Johnny's face crumpled even more. 'But it's not time yet. She's not of age. She needs all her power to win. If Morrigan gets hold of Raine's Glimmer, she'll be invincible! What are we going to do?'

'You'll have to go down there. I can't leave the Gateway, it's too weak. Anything could get through.'

Johnny's head swam. His feet were lead weights, which would make walking tricky. Luckily, you didn't get to where he was going by walking.

Elsie unrolled the carpet she had dragged down the alley. She tapped it with her white wand. The rug rose and hovered in the air. She tipped Johnny, with his light head and heavy feet, on to the rug. It quivered like a racehorse.

A large figure on four stumpy legs blundered out of a nearby shadowed doorway. It threw itself with a thud onto the flying carpet. Johnny patted his faithful bag. They rose unsteadily, the air shimmered, and with a crack like thunder, they were gone.

CHAPTER 9
BABE IN THE WOODS

Monkey said that all primates, which included Raine, and would she please try to concentrate, had an excellent sense of direction. He was sure cutting straight through the woods would take them directly to the Crystal Mountain. They had to follow the sun. Raine swung a strong branch she'd found like a club, attacking vines that stretched out onto the path and wrapped around her legs.

'Monkey?'

'Yeah?' Monkey perched on her shoulders, ducking under overhanging branches that tried to whip their faces like pointy, wooden fingers. Little Thirty-Five was curled up in her bag, snoring. Wafts of smoke crept out of the bag and snaked up Raine's arm to settle in her nostrils.

'Is there something a bit weird about these trees? I hit a branch out of the way, and I think it said "ow." Look at this.' Raine raised her stick and walloped a tree trunk. Its branches shook and its leaves rustled. 'There's no wind. Why's it moving?'

'I dunno. Ignore it. Trees can't feel things.'

'But this one's got a face.' Raine poked a wide, short tree with her stick. Its trunk was knotted and twisted. Two whorls were angry eyes and a slash across the trunk was a thin-lipped mouth. Dark, shiny leaves hung down like hair over a forehead. She poked it again.

'Monkey, that tree growled at me!'

Monkey rapped on her head with his knuckles. 'Stop mucking about with bits of wood! It doesn't matter! Look at the sun, Raine!'

They had been walking for hours. The orange sun hung ahead of them, instead of above, skimming the green treetops. Sweat trickled down Raine's back. She didn't want to be stuck in this creepy wood at dusk, but when she thought about the Crystal Mountain she felt sick.

'Come on then,' she muttered, pulling bits of weed off her legs that had curled around her ankles while they were talking. She set off down the path again. The undergrowth near her feet rustled. A branch snapped behind her. She slowed. There was something not very nice about this wood. The sweat on her back cooled and tickled her spine like icy fingers.

'What's that?' She pointed at a round bush. 'I saw something red in there. Two things. Glowing red. In that bush.' The bush was still. The forest was quiet.

'Well, there is a chance, I suppose, that we've crossed over from the Enchanted Wood into the Dark Forest,' Monkey said. 'Which means we should start hurrying and not be here when it gets dark.'

'When it gets dark in the Dark Forest? That doesn't sound fun.' It was bad enough now. Raine wasn't going to find out what might happen if she was still on this path when the sun went down. Adventures weren't exciting like she'd always imagined. They were scary, and sweaty, and made your feet hurt from walking too far. At least she had Monkey to keep her company. She was even getting used to the constant whiff of Little Thirty-Five's smoky burps. It would be much worse if she was all alone.

Raine walked on, although she did stop hitting the trees and tried to step over the branches that blocked her feet instead of knocking them out of the way with her stick.

She tried to ignore another noise coming from among the trees and carried on walking. But there it was again. A faint mew, like an animal in pain. Raine paused, her tree branch in mid-swing. Yes, there was something in the bushes up ahead. Her fingers tightened around her stick. What if Scary Fairy was back? She should block the sound out and keep moving. She looked up at the red ball hanging low in the sky. There was no time to spare. She squared her shoulders and stood up straight. She was on a quest after all. But there it was again – a sad, pathetic mewling.

'Did you hear that, Monkey?'

'Umm. Yes,' he said.

'What do you think it was?' she asked.

'The wind?'

Raine shook her head. It was no good. She couldn't ignore it, or pretend it was the wind. After all, she was supposed to be good! She crept off the path, picking her way through the undergrowth. Once they were standing in front of the bush where the sound seemed to be coming from, Monkey slipped from her shoulders. He hid behind Raine's legs. She used the stick to separate some leaves and peered at the bottom of the bush. There, lying on the dirt, was a baby with a mop of black hair hanging over its forehead.

'I don't think babies are supposed to be blue. We've got to help.'

Raine's mother had found a kitten once and had put it inside her jumper to keep it warm. Bruiser had made them give it away of course, but she'd saved its life. Raine dropped her stick, picked up the baby with a grunt and cuddled it to her chest. The baby was so cold, it must have been left out in the elements for ages. She backed out from the bush, holding the baby close. It was too heavy, and its legs hung down to her knees. It wasn't moving, and it had stopped crying. Its breath whistled in and out.

'What are we going to do with that?' Monkey asked.

'I suppose we should light a fire, see if we can warm it up a bit. Can you get some wood?'

Monkey looked up at the sky and shook his head. 'I don't think we've got time. It's getting late, and we don't want to be here at nightfall. You thought the fairy children were bad? Well...'

A squeak vibrated in Raine's ear, 'Why don't you

use those colour things that follow you around everywhere?' Little Thirty-Five stretched and yawned, pouring a waft of smoke straight into Raine's face. Tears trickled down her cheeks.

'What colours? What are you talking about?'

'Those shiny, sparkly things that come off you. All the time.' Little Thirty-Five pointed his claw at Raine's head. 'There. And there.'

Raine closed her eyes. As usual, she had no idea what was going on, or what to do. What was Little Thirty-Five talking about? Magic colours coming off her head? She thought back to when all this weirdness started. Uncle Johnny. He'd held her hand and she'd broken that window with something coming out of her finger. Had that been a magic colour? It had! She'd seen a blue spark fly out of her finger.

She opened her eyes and glared at Monkey.

'What do you know about this? I broke that window with some blue stuff that came out of my finger. And when I touched that old rug, it lit up.' Raine trailed off. There had been something else weird in the basement too. 'And when I put my hand on her newspaper, the letters changed over into English. I thought Bruiser shook my brain about. But those weren't Dutch words. And that wasn't an ordinary rug.' The breath got stuck in her chest. She let it out with a whoosh, 'Those are *magic* words, aren't they?'

Monkey stopped trying to pull the buttons off his waistcoat.

'Yep. And those colours are your Glimmer. It's untamed magic.'

The hot, angry feeling bubbled under Raine's skin again. Why didn't anyone *ever* tell her *anything?* She scowled at Monkey with lava boiling through her veins. Her bag oozed even more warmth into her thigh. The book wanted to tell her something. At least *something* was being helpful. She took the weight of the heavy, sleeping baby in one arm. With the other she opened the bag flap and lifted the book out. It opened on the very first page. There, on the inside cover was a heart drawn in red pen.

There'd never been anything like that in the book before. She was sure. She ran her thumb over the writing. EM would be Mum – Elsie Major, but who was MM?

She slipped the book back into her bag. Her fingers fumbled around inside. Where was the feather? She groaned. She'd managed to lose the one thing that might have helped.

The baby was far too heavy to hold one-handed for long.

'Monkey? What's going on? Why does Mum have so much weird stuff?'

'I'm not allowed to tell you anything. It's The Lore.'

Raine laughed, but she didn't mean it. None of this was funny. Confusing and scary, but not funny.

'The law? What, you'll get arrested for telling me stuff?'

Monkey gulped at the darkening sky.

'Worse. Screechers.'

'What?' Raine was beginning to annoy herself. 'What?' was her new favourite word, but it didn't matter how many times she asked it – nothing made sense.

'I can't tell you anything because it's against The Lore and if I do your grandfa— I mean The Grand

Magus will send Screechers after me and I'll be put into The Dark and I'll never come back!' Monkey wailed and hid his face in his paws. His shoulders shook.

Little Thirty-Five fluttered up to him and stroked the top of his head with a leathery wing. 'Why did you make him cry? I thought he's your friend!'

'He is! I didn't mean to!' Raine shifted under the weight of the baby. She wouldn't be able to carry it for much longer. The last thing she needed was for her friend to have a nervous breakdown in the middle of Spooky Wood or whatever it was called. She'd have to ignore emotional monkeys, magic books, grumpy trees, and glowing red things in bushes that looked like eyes following you.

They'd wasted enough time already, and she didn't fancy hanging around to see what the night forest had in store for them.

'Sorry, Monkey. It's not your fault. Let's help this really, really big and heavy baby and go and save the world.' Maybe if she sounded brave, she'd end up feeling brave. 'Give me your waistcoat, please.'

Monkey grinned and unbuttoned his vest. Once it was off, he handed it over to Raine. She wrapped it in the soft material. Then she closed her eyes and summoned all the peaceful blue light she could feel. She searched for the pool of cool, calm water the stone man had poured into her. She pictured a blue glow wrapping around her and the baby. When she opened her eyes again, Monkey and Little Thirty-Five were holding onto each other and staring. They were enveloped in a glowing blue light. Its healing waves streamed out from her.

The baby stirred, snuggling in closer to Raine. Monkey crept closer, settling in a low tree branch behind Raine. Little Thirty-Five settled on top of Raine's head, snagging his claws in her hair. The blue light pulsed, and the baby turned pink. It's lank, dark hair pinged up into curls and stood up around its head. Suddenly, the baby opened a single eye in the middle of its forehead and stared straight at Raine. The blue light pulsed once more and died.

Monkey crept forward. 'It's a cyclops!' he whispered. 'They're really rare! I've only heard of them, never seen one!'

The baby fixed her in an intense stare from its single eye.

'It's not evil, is it?' Raine whispered to Monkey, out of the corner of her mouth.

'Is it pretty?' Monkey asked.

Raine cooed at the baby and rocked it up and down. 'Only to its mother.'

'Well then, we're probably safe.'

The baby stared into Raine's eyes. Tickly fingers probed her brain. *This again.* People should ask before they go scrabbling about inside your head. She waited for the images to appear that meant someone was sending her thoughts. A picture formed – a settlement of roughly built circular mud huts, with branches and leaves for roofs. A huge woman dressed in animal skins sat cross-legged outside one of the huts. She held her head in her hands, a mass of tangled black hair trailing over her shoulders.

'I think it wants us to take it back to its mother.'

Monkey groaned.

'We can't leave it here, can we?'

'And how are we supposed to find her? It's a baby. It can't talk, can it?' He scoffed at the creature. 'Can you?'

The baby opened its mouth. Raine nearly dropped it when an old man's rasping voice said, 'Yes, I can. I will show you the way.'

The baby shut its eye and put its head on Raine's shoulder. While Raine and Monkey were still wondering what they were supposed to do, it started snoring. A picture flashed in Raine's mind. She knew how to get to the cyclops' home; a map jumped into her head and her feet pointed where to go.

'Come on, it's this way. Not far!' She marched off, twigs cracking under her feet. *Sorry, trees.*

Monkey called behind her. 'Raine! You're heading away from the Crystal Mountain! You're going deeper into the forest!' She didn't turn around. She couldn't be a hero by leaving a baby to die. Monkey would have to get over it and catch up.

CHAPTER 10
ONE-EYED BANDITS

Raine hovered at the edge of a clearing. Around its perimeter was a circle of round mud huts. As Raine was deciding whether to enter the camp, a massive brown boot came hurtling out of the nearest hut. She ducked and it sailed over her head. It was followed by an enormous clay pot that broke into pieces at her feet. Giants ran about, waving wooden clubs around and screaming at each other.

In the middle of the village there was a hut bigger than the others, with a fire burning outside its entrance. An animal skin with red shapes painted on it hung over the doorway. The cyclops from Raine's vision sat outside the hut, her head in her hands.

Raine dithered at the edge of the clearing for a

moment, the resting baby snoring against her chest. Little Thirty-Five's claws pinched her shoulder where he perched like a featherless, smelly parrot. Monkey had better not be far behind. The enormous woman sitting by the fire swung her head up and stared straight at Raine with a single, cloudy eye. The woman bellowed and another cyclops came running. He helped her up and they clomped towards Raine. The male cyclops stared at her with his big, blue eye, but Raine was pinned to the ground by the strange-eyed woman's gaze.

Silence fell. Every giant stopped what they were doing and turned to Raine. Dressed in animal furs, with plaited and braided hair, or shaved heads, each cyclops had a single eye in the middle of their forehead, some blue, like the baby's, others brown like Raine's eyes, trained on her and shining like a lamp in the looming dusk. They gathered around the two cyclops in front of Raine, towering over them. The two cyclops were much shorter than the others. Did you get dwarf giants? It didn't matter, they were all much bigger than her. They could squash her like an ant.

'Umm. Hello?' Raine warbled.

She looked around for Monkey. Where was he? He'd better hurry up.

The woman reached out and grabbed the baby. 'Gigan!' she said to the other short cyclops, 'She found Dad!'

Raine blinked. Dad? Why was she calling a baby Dad? The book got warm, but now wasn't a great time to sit down and have a bit of a read.

'Umm. I can't really stay! Got a... err, a mission to do, so umm... glad you got your baby back!'

A heavy hand landed on her shoulder. The woman propelled Raine towards the centre of the camp. The hand pressed Raine down to the ground until she was sitting cross-legged in front of the fire. The flames were too hot after her stumble through the forest. Sweat pooled under her arms and in her hair. The woman put the baby back in Raine's arms and pulled aside the dried animal hide strung in front of the door to her hut. She disappeared inside. The rest of the cyclopes drifted towards Raine and sat down in a wide semicircle on the other side of the fire. No one spoke.

Where was Monkey? She could make a run for it, but she didn't know which way to go. She sat sweating and watching the sky darken.

The cyclops clumped from her tent, carrying a foaming, smoking cup. *No way!* Raine wasn't accepting any drinks from anyone. She'd learned that lesson the hard way.

The cyclops sat down next to Raine. She took the baby and held the frothing cup under his nose. The baby's eye blinked open. It opened its mouth. The woman poured the liquid down its throat. The cyclops held the baby up over her shoulder and patted its back a few times. It burped.

'You saved my dad,' the woman said in a high-pitched voice, 'and so, you have saved all of the cyclops. Thank you.'

'That's not really a baby?' Raine eyed the strange creature as it hiccupped. 'I thought you were its mum.' Raine looked again at the cyclops. 'But you're a kid too, aren't you? Like me.'

The baby giggled. All the other cyclops laughed too. Great. Somehow, she'd made an idiot out of herself.

The girl smiled at Raine. At least she wasn't laughing at her. 'No, he's not a baby. He's Specto – the Seer. I'm Tantulum, his daughter, and this,' she nodded to the other short cyclops, 'is Gigan, my brother. You can call me Tantu. When we cyclopes age, we enter a second childhood. We go back to our infant state as we approach death.'

'You mean you get younger instead of older?'

'Yes. It's his time.' Tantu's enormous shoulders shook. Her white eye filled with tears. 'Dad's dying.'

Poor Tantu. Finally, here was something Raine understood. She'd lost her dad too. Even though she didn't really know him, she'd always felt a connection. But now even that was gone. Dads shouldn't die when their kids were just kids. It wasn't fair. She knew how Tantu felt. Like the bottom was dropping out of her world. She'd like to hug her, but she reached out and patted Tantu's massive arm instead.

'I'm sorry,' Raine whispered.

Specto wriggled and Tantu set him on her lap. 'As we age, we become helpless, and we must rely on the Clan to look after us.' The old man voice coming from a baby made the skin on Raine's head tighten up and prickle. Why was everything in this world so strange? Just when she thought she was starting to get a grip on things, it all went upside down and back to front again. Little Thirty-Five whimpered in her ear, hiding in a curl of hair. She reached up and patted him.

'So, why was he under the bushes? That's not being very well looked after, is it?' Raine asked Tantu, the old man baby snoring again.

'The Queen of Chaos.'

Raine's stomach flipped. She knew that name. The sorceress. If only she still had the feather in her bag. After all, it had been a wand once. Wasn't she going to need a wand to fight a witch?

'Only one cyclops in each generation has the gift of the Sight; Dad is this Clan's Seer. When he dies, his sight will pass on to me. Without the Sight, we can't communicate with other Clans, and we can't know the past or the future.'

'What do you mean, you can't know the past?' Raine wasn't sure how much more of today her brain could take.

'A cyclops has no memory of his own. We only have a Clan memory, which is held within the Seer. And he spreads that memory among the family. If he dies away from the family, those memories die with him, and so does the Sight. He needs to be here for me to inherit the gift.'

'And then you'll be able to see?'

'Yeah, my eye will clear – all Seers are blind until they inherit the Sight. Until then Gigan is my eyes.'

'So, what was he doing, umm...' Raine's cheeks burned, '*naked* in the forest?'

'The Queen of Chaos...' Movement rippled around the fire. The Cyclops gestured in the air before tapping their foreheads three times. Tantu ignored them. 'She knows how powerful we are in battle – I mean, look at us! We're built for war!' It was true. Raine wouldn't mind being backed up by this lot. They were all *huge* and swung those massive wooden clubs like twigs. Each one rippled with muscles from their massive sloping shoulders down to their hairy calves.

'She also knows that without our Seer, we'd be useless... we wouldn't be able to find the other Clans. Morrigan's spies stalk this forest. One of them must have warned her Dad is close to death. She crept into our camp at night and stole him. She abandoned him in the forest to die. He managed to send out some memory to me. That's why we were still looking for him.'

Tantu cocked her head to one side. Her sightless eye stared right into Raine. It made her toes curl. 'What's wrong?'

'You said her spies stalk the forest... and I can't find Monkey. And I can't feel him with my mind. Do you think he's okay?'

'I don't know, Princess. The creature's only

connection is with you, and he's not a cyclops so I can't reach out to him. I can see if Dad can call to the other Clans and see if anyone has seen or heard of him, if you like?'

Raine nodded. Monkey wouldn't have wandered off, would he? What about those glowing red circles she'd spotted moving through the bushes in the forest? She should have paid more attention.

Tantu put her forehead against Specto's and shut her eye for a few minutes that dragged like hours to Raine watching the sun set. Tantu frowned.

'What?' Raine demanded. 'Is he alright?'

Tantu shook her head 'The Clans don't know. No one has seen him travel through the forest. But they told me The Queen of Chaos has gathered her forces. There are thousands of them! Hordes of Screechers!'

Raine gulped. Her hands clenched into fists so tight her nails gouged into her palms. Monkey had said something about Screechers. It was the only time since she'd met him that he'd been afraid.

'The dragons are there, with the other creatures of light. They've gathered on the slopes of the Crystal Mountain – but the enemy are too many! She's hiding in the forest with them. The Army of Light has no idea how many they face! It's hopeless!'

Raine dug her fingers into the dry ground underneath her. Her head span and her stomach lurched up into her throat – there had to be something she could do! If only the dragons could breathe fire, they'd stand a chance. But she didn't have a clue how to help.

She grabbed the book out of her bag. She'd let it fall open and hope for the best. *Please work.* The book was cold in her hands. It's cover dull grey in the murky light. She opened it to a blank page. She riffled through the pages – they were all blank. She resisted the urge to throw the stupid book in the fire. What was she going to do?

Little Thirty-Five crept out from his hiding spot in her hair and peered down at the book.

'That's a bit weird, isn't it?' he burped at her. Eye watering smoke curled up her nostrils and tickled her brain. *Of course! If Little Thirty-Five can fart fire, so can the other dragons!*

She scooped Little Thirty-Five up in her hand. They stared at each other.

'What?'

'How brave are you, Little Thirty-Five?'

He stood up to his full height and stretched his wings out. 'Super brave. What do you need me to do?'

A few minutes later he flapped out of the camp as fast as his little wings could flap.

Raine turned to Tantu. If Little Thirty-Five was brave enough to fly off through the Dark Forest all by himself, she had to be brave too. 'How far are we from the Crystal Mountain?'

'You'll never make it there alone by sundown, Princess, and that's when she'll strike. Some of her army need to stay sheltered in the dark; they won't come out from the shadows while the sun is in the sky.'

'What's the quickest way for me to get there? I can call Little One, the dragon. He can come and get me, and we can fly to the Mountain!'

'There's no time, even for that.' Gigan bent down and whispered in Tantu's ear. She nodded and he lumbered up to Raine. The earth shook. She tried to smile at him while ignoring the enormous nail-studded club in his hand.

'It's settled!' Tantu pointed at her brother. 'Gigan will take you to the Crystal Mountain.'

'And how will following a cyclops get me there in time?'

Tantu reached out and held Raine's hand. 'No. You'll ride on Gigan's shoulders. He'll run through the forest. There's a chance he can get you there before it's too late. He's the fastest cyclops here.'

Tantu put the baby down. She lifted Raine up by her collar and dumped her on Gigan's shoulders. He stood, and the ground disappeared from beneath them. Raine shrieked and gripped hard onto the only thing she could find to hold onto – Gigan's sticky-out ears. Gigan turned in a circle and broke into a run. He loped away with Raine bouncing up and down on his shoulders and hanging onto his ears.

Tantu's voice echoed in her head as they raced off. 'We'll follow you. May the Light be with you!' Raine's hands tightened on Gigan's ears. *What if the light isn't with me?* Her head span. *What if I'm too late?*

CHAPTER II
A TROLL WITH A DIFFERENCE

There might only be one Gigan, but riding on his shoulders felt like being in the middle of a herd of stampeding elephants. Saplings, raising their spindly arms up towards the sky got trampled under his thundering feet. Trees had branches ripped from their trunks. Raine did her best to ignore the muttering following behind them.

Even though Monkey had said trees don't have feelings, she got the sense she'd made the woods cross earlier with her stick. Using a cyclops to mow them down wouldn't make her any friends with the Dark Forest. The Dark Army, on the other hand, had most likely lived there since the dawn of time. Evil creatures, all red eyes and pointy talons, could be hiding right now, watching as she crashed through their home. *What if it's them I can hear?*

'Ow! My ears.'

Raine's knuckles were white. Gigan's ears were not. They were bright red and sore looking. She took a deep breath and loosened her too tight grip.

'Sorry, Gigan. I'm a bit stressed.'

They reached a huge tree with a knotted trunk. Its branches stretched out over a slow moving, brown river. Gigan slowed and skidded to a stop in front of an old, stone bridge. A long, spiky, scratchy finger slipped down the back of Raine's jacket. It lifted her off Gigan's shoulders and into the muddy river.

Raine sat up, spluttering and spitting out a mouthful of slimy grey weed. It tasted quite nice – sort of lemony. But she wasn't in the mood to stop and think about the wonders of this frustrating world. She struggled to the shore and reached out to grab a low hanging branch to pull herself up the riverbank. The branch shook her off with a rustle of its leaves and she landed back in the water with a splash.

Gigan reached out an immense arm and plucked her out of the water.

'Did that tree dunk me in the river? And push me back in again?' Raine asked, shaking herself like a dog and glaring at the tree. It rustled its leaves. She was sure she could hear sniggering.

Gigan shrugged. He was staring at the bridge, his eye looking even bigger than usual.

'Sorry, Princess,' he muttered in an earthshaking boom. 'Cyclops is scared of two things: water and trolls.'

'Gigan.' Raine tried to arrange her face into a patient, kind expression. 'It's okay, we'll pop over the bridge. It'll be fine – I'll hold your hand if you like.'

The cyclops peered at the shadowy space under the bridge. 'No troll? You promise, Princess?'

Raine clenched her jaw. She mustn't lose her temper. It was like being nursemaid to a giant toddler. She sighed.

'No, Gigan, no troll. I promise.'

Raine stretched up and grabbed Gigan by his little finger. She pulled him towards the bridge.

She put her foot on the first stone. A voice boomed out, 'HALT! WHO GOES THERE?'

Gigan's finger slipped out of her hand. The cyclops

let out an, 'Eek!' and lifting the hem of his tunic between his thumbs and forefingers, ran away on tiptoes. He took cover behind the big tree that had dumped Raine in the river. He peered over the tree's canopy and squeaked, 'Troll!' before ducking down and peering out through the tree's branches.

What the heck? They were never going to make it to the Crystal Mountain. She picked up a large fallen branch lying by her foot.

The deep voice echoed out from under the bridge again, 'WHO DARES TO INTERRUPT MY REST?'

Whoever the voice belonged to sounded big. And cross.

Raine's heartbeat thundered in her ears like a drum. Her hands tightened around her branch until her arms shook. Her jaw clenched and she ground her teeth.

'I don't have time for this!' she screamed at the troll under the bridge. 'I don't know who you are! I don't care! Do you know who *I* am?' The sun dropped lower and dusk crept closer to dark. Raine stamped her feet and pounded the earth with her branch. Her muscles screamed. The drum pounded in her ears. Why couldn't she cross the bridge without all this drama? How was she going to get to the Crystal

Mountain in time now?

'Do you know who *I* am?'

Gigan crept out from behind his tree and came to stand beside her.

There was a crunching, like big feet on small stones, from under the bridge. The voice spoke out again, less booming, less deep. 'Err. No?'

At the far side of the bridge, a squat, green bush swished. A gruff voice spoke from its green depths.

'*I* know who you are,' said the bush.

Raine dropped her stick. She rubbed her face with dirty hands. *What now?*

A square, red bottom wiggled its way out of the bush, followed by a round body and a messy, leaf-strewn head.

'I know who you are,' it repeated as it turned around, revealing itself to be a plump dwarf with a big, red nose and a long, brown beard tucked into its belt. It stomped its way to the middle of the bridge where it stood with its arms folded across its barrel chest.

'I know who *that* is too,' it said with a nod down towards the bridge under its feet. It raised its voice. 'It's not a troll! It's a very naughty dwarf!'

Indistinct muttering floated out from under the bridge. It didn't matter. Whatever was happening here, she needed to get across.

Raine addressed the dwarf on the bridge, 'Ummm. Excuse me, Sir—'

The dwarf on the bridge snorted and glared. The thing under the bridge giggled.

The dwarf scowled and leaned further out over the bridge. 'And if it doesn't come out from under there *right now*, its Mummy is going to be very cross and send it to bed without any supper!'

The thing under the bridge wailed, 'Oh, Mum!' followed by scrabbling and grunting. A tiny pair of hands appeared on the edge of the bridge. A small brown boot swung up over the edge and another dwarf, very similar to the first, but half the height and with a much less impressive beard clambered up.

The first dwarf strode forward and grabbed the smaller dwarf by its ear. 'What did I tell you about trying to frighten those poor cyclopes, Lucky?'

'Sorry, Mum!' the little dwarf squeaked as it was shaken about by the ear.

Enough. Bad manners or not, Raine had to interrupt this family meeting.

'Umm, excuse me! Hello!' she called over the bridge, 'I, uh, I excuse me – I have to get across here now!'

The mother dwarf let go of her told-off child and tucked her beard back in her belt.

'Oh yes, right. That.'

Raine stamped her feet. She kicked the bridge. She tangled her fingers in her messy hair and pulled until hurt. *The world's about to end, and everyone will blame me. I can' t even cross a bridge.*

'Excuse me, Mrs Dwarf!' Raine bellowed. 'If you and your son—' The mother dwarf hissed and the little dwarf howled. Raine ploughed on, 'If you and your... daughter could kindly move out of the way. I NEED TO SAVE THE WORLD! IF YOU DON'T MIND!'

The mother dwarf stood stony-faced, probably used to dealing with childish tantrums, even if Raine did stand a good a couple of feet taller than her.

'Yes, dear, I know. That's what the fat man said. And I do have a name. You may call me Mrs Battalax.'

'What fat man?'

'The one in the dress. And the pointy hat. With the licky bag.'

Raine untangled her fingers and pulled her

rumpled tunic down. She must look a sight. She coughed behind her fist. Her throat burned from all the shouting.

It had to be Uncle Johnny. Maybe Mum had sent him. He'd take her home and she could forget this whole bizarre adventure. She could have cried. Instead, Raine grasped Gigan's hand and pulled him onto the stone bridge.

'Take me to him!' she commanded in her best royal voice.

Gigan reached the middle of the bridge. The little dwarf said, 'Boo!' Gigan fell off into the river, dragging Raine with him.

***

Deep under the forest, Raine followed Mrs Battalax through a series of twisting damp tunnels carved out of the rock. The dwarf carried a smoking torch in her hand, dimly glowing against the glistening walls. Raine, bent double, stumbled along in a half-run trying to keep up with the little woman striding ahead. Sharp stones dug into her feet. The constant prattle of the child dwarf followed close on her heels.

'My best friend's Ducky, but not really 'cause one

time when we were runnin' in the tunnels and I fell down, he left me, so really I like Linky best, and she's got the best hammer, one time when we found a line of lead in the iron, she let me use it and I bashed my thumb and it went all massive and red...' The words droned on and on, washing over her like a wave, until one word caught in Raine's ear. The dwarf crashed into her and tumbled to the stone floor as she stopped suddenly.

'Did you say lead?' Raine asked, helping the dwarf to her feet.

'Yeah, course. Mum says where there's iron, there's always lead.'

Raine had watched *Snow White and the Seven Dwarves* at a friend's house before Bruiser had banned her from visiting her friends. The story was also in her mum's book. At least it had been, before it went weird and came alive. The book rested against her hip. It was cold. Why wasn't it helping her anymore? She'd lost Monkey, she'd lost the feather, she'd sent Little Thirty-Five away, and her book had decided to go unhelpfully normal again. She needed to face the fact that she was by herself, with no one and nothing else to rely on. Could she fulfil the prophecy? She'd have to.

Raine looked down at the dwarf, who had pulled out a chisel from goodness knows where. She was filing her nails with it.

'Are you miners? You mine iron? And lead?'

The little dwarf rolled her eyes at Raine as if it was the most stupid question she'd ever heard.

'Yeah, course. We're *dwarves.*'

'What do you do with it?' What had Mrs Battalax called her child on the bridge? Clunky? Blinky? 'Slinky? What do you do with the lead?'

The little dwarf bristled. 'Linky's my best friend. I'm Lucky. And we make it into coins. And we make the iron into weapons. And we make the copper and silver into plates and cups and stuff. Why?'

'Just interested. Have you got any coins? To have a look.' The book had said something about lead. If only it would warm her skin and give her a sign she was on the right track.

Lucky reached down the front of her trousers and wriggled. A second later she pulled out a small brown pouch and handed it over to Raine. It was very warm, Raine didn't want to think about where it had been kept.

Lucky shrugged. 'What? Got no pockets. You can

keep that, by the way. I've got heaps of money.' Raine slipped the clinking pouch into her bag, next to the cold book.

'CHILDREN! *Will you stop DITHERING!*' Mrs Battalax's loud voice echoed from around the corner. Raine and Lucky bolted after her.

Raine clonked her head on a stalactite hanging from the ceiling like a pointy finger. Her feet slipped on the loose stones. She tripped over Lucky and rolled down the tunnel. When the stars cleared from her eyes, she was lying in the doorway to a little stone room with a coal fire burning in the centre. A vast shadow loomed up the side of the room, long fingers twisting themselves together.

'Flippin' cold down here. Right in my bones.' Uncle Johnny held his chubby fingers over the fire, their shadow twins scampering up the wall. He cocked his head at Raine.

'You're wet. Come in then, no time to dawdle.'

Rubbing her temple, the bruise a lump under her fingers, Raine took a small step and then hurtled to Uncle Johnny. She buried herself in his welcoming hug; he smelt of sweat and cigars. She wasn't going to bury herself, after all.

'Oh, Uncle Johnny, I've lost Monkey!' The words

came out as a wail. Before she knew it, she was blubbering into his armpit, her breath hitching. *Was deodorant against wizards' rules?*

She sobbed out her whole story, from the moment she kicked her way out of the basement to just now, when she'd banged her head on the stalactite. Uncle Johnny rubbed her forehead while she spoke. The pain faded and her wet clothes dried. Her body tingled, and a warm feeling flooded through her. Raine stopped crying, stood up and wiped her face on her sleeve. She wriggled her toes. Even her shoes were dry.

'Oh, sorry. I'm standing on your dress.'

'It's not a dress, it's a robe. All wizards have them. It's tradition.'

'I see. Well, it's very pretty.'

Johnny chuckled. 'You sound like your mum. She had a smart mouth on her too. Smart mouth, smart brain. Like you. You can do this you know, Raine, you're your mother's daughter after all.'

'What's this got to do with Mum?' Raine wiped her snotty, tear-stained face on a corner of Uncle Johnny's long robe. 'I thought this was about my dad. Isn't that why I'm here, because I'm his daughter? I mean, I know I'm Mum's daughter, but she's just

Mum...' Raine slipped her hand in her bag. Cold. 'Uncle Johnny, she hasn't always been just Mum, has she?'

'Nope.'

'Right.' Of course, she wasn't – she had a basement full of weird stuff that changed when you touched it, and a magic book. And if she had all that stuff, she might even have a wand.

'She's a witch, isn't she? My boring old mum is actually a witch,' she said. It had sounded crazy in Raine's head, and it sounded crazy when she said it out loud. It was a *stupid* idea.

'If she's a witch, why are we are we so poor, and live in Scutter's Alley with Bruiser? She must be a totally rubbish witch if she couldn't even get us out of that! And why didn't she save my dad?' Raine screwed up the hem of her top between her hands. 'It's all her fault,' she said.

'No, you stop that, my girl. She kept you safe. No one else could have hidden you for so long.' Johnny's eyebrows lowered and his forehead creased. 'Greatest witch there ever was.' He paused. 'Well, one of them, anyway.'

'So, my dad is a dead prince in another world, and my mum is a witch who lives in the yuckiest place ever, with a mean bully and never does any magic? But that's okay because she was keeping me safe?'

Johnny nodded. 'Well, that's the short version, Raine, but yes, you've got the gist of it.' He kneeled next to Raine and put his hands on her shoulders. 'There are reasons for it all, I promise. But there's no time for me to tell you. It's your mum's story anyway, not mine. You're her daughter, and you have her power. Now you need to use it.'

Raine could scream. 'She doesn't have any power! Bruiser yells at her all the time! And he hates me! And our house is cold, and there's never enough food! What kind of a witch would she be if she let all that happen? She's not strong, she's weak!'

Johnny sighed. 'Your mum was one of the best witches I've ever met, one of the best two, in fact. She could have been the Grande Dame when your grandfather steps down—'

'What's the Grande Dame? Hang on, I've got a *granddad?*'

'But she met your dad and turned her back on all that. Swore off magicking and settled down to be your mum.'

'Yeah, but Dad's dead! And why couldn't she turn Bruiser into a frog or something?'

Johnny ran his fingers through his messy brown hair. 'She did something – or rather she wouldn't do something, so the Inner Circle decreed that—'

'The inner what?'

Johnny hauled himself to his feet. 'No. No more interruptions. You can ask all the questions you want afterwards. Your mother was supposed to do something. She didn't. It was decreed that she could no longer practise magic, and she was sent to be a Guardian.'

'Of me? My guardian? Because I'm a witch? With a Glimmer thingy?'

'No. Of the Gateway, a place where worlds meet. Or try to. She's a gatekeeper, there to ensure nothing gets through from either side.'

'I got through.'

'Yes, well, you're a halfling. Half-witch, half-creature of light. You're even more powerful than your mother was. More powerful than we realised.' Johnny bent down and looked Raine in the eyes. 'And that's why you have to go. Now.' He nodded his head towards a tatty looking rug lying on the floor, which rippled suddenly and lifted its front like a dog sitting up on its back legs. 'You'll fly on that.'

Raine opened her mouth, to find Johnny's finger held against her lips. It smelt like tobacco and salt and vinegar crisps.

'No. No more questions. You'll fly. It isn't hard — it was your mum's first learner carpet. The dwarves and I will follow through the tunnels and pray to the Light we get there in time to be of any use to you.'

It was all too much. Yesterday she'd been Drippy Raine, skulking around Scutter's Alley and moaning because life was boring, and today she was a magical witchy-princess. Her mum was a witch, a powerful one, which must run in the family because Raine's granddad was apparently some sort of big magic thingy too.

Had Monkey nearly told her back in the forest when he'd been scared about Screechers? Something about a Grand Magus? There wasn't enough room for all these thoughts; her head was going to explode. But she didn't feel like screaming anymore.

Maybe Johnny was right, and her mum didn't have a choice, like Raine didn't have a choice now. She had to go and march into battle against another powerful witch, whether she wanted to or not.

How many witches and wizards were there out in the world? Mum was one, her grandfather was one and *she* was one, and now she had to go and fight one. Her brain itched. She was sure she was missing something important. And if Morrigan was so powerful, why hadn't she tried to take over the world before? What had she been doing creeping about in some damp, dingy wood for the last ten years?

If Raine was an evil witch, she'd be swanning around in silks and jewels and living in a fancy castle. It didn't make sense, like it didn't make sense that her mum was a witch who used to be married to a prince and now lived in Scutter's Alley. And what did Bruiser have to do with it? It didn't add up.

'Uncle Johnny?'

'Mmmm?' Uncle Johnny was scratching a green bag that looked like it would be wagging its tail if it had one. It ran over on stumpy tan coloured legs and butted Raine behind the knees. Then it dropped to the floor and rolled on its back.

'He wants to you to tickle his tummy.'

Raine bent down and scratched the bag. A long, smooth, pink tongue shot out and licked her hand, leaving it covered in slobber. Raine laughed, wiping her hand on her trousers. 'What's its name?'

'BagDog. Not to be confused with bad dog. He's a good boy.' Johnny roughly tickled the bag. It wriggled across the floor with its long pink tongue lolling on to the stone floor. 'Are you ready to go now, Raine? It's time.'

'I suppose.' She wasn't, not really. Her palms were sticky with sweat, and a bit of BagDog saliva. Her heart was beating too fast, like it might jump out of her chest and run away. 'Do you think they're okay? The dragons, and everyone else, and Little Thirty-Five?'

Johnny shrugged. 'Why don't you have a quick look? It's probably the only chance you'll have to practise a bit of magic before you meet *her* – can't hurt. All you need is a reflective surface like a mirror, or water.'

'We're in a cave. Made of rock. There's nothing shiny in here. It's all,' Raine looked around, 'rocky.'

A head popped out from a shadowed ledge above Johnny. 'I know where there's something shiny.' Lucky dropped down to the floor. 'I'll show you, c'mon.'

She grabbed Raine by the hand and pulled her towards a narrow tunnel. Raine ducked her head and let Lucky drag her along. Johnny folded himself in half and followed, BagDog trundling along at his heels. The carpet fluttered in the air and then floated into the passageway.

Lucky stopped in front of a big, round boulder plonked right in the middle of the floor.

'Ta da!' she announced with her arms spread wide.

Raine ran her hand over the rock. It was cold and smooth. But it wasn't shiny.

'No. There.' Lucky pointed with her chisel at the top of the rock. 'See?'

Raine peered closer. Lucky was right, there was a glint in the rock. She rubbed her thumb over the patch. Dust fell away and a purple glow lit up her hand.

'What is it?' She rubbed her hand over sharp angles and smooth surfaces. 'Is it a jewel? What's it doing in this rock?'

'Dunno. I tried chipping it out.' Lucky waggled her chisel at the rock and glared at it, 'But it wouldn't let me. I cut my thumb. Dwarves *never* cut themselves mining.'

Raine slumped against the rock. Its cold seeped into her side. If a dwarf couldn't get the jewel out, how was she supposed to? She should forget about it and get to the Crystal Mountain. She'd have to see when she got there if anyone was still alive.

Stupid rock. She stood up and slapped it. The rock

crumbled into dust, making a huge grey pile at her feet. A sword with a gleaming purple stone set in its hilt lay on top. A line of writing ran along its blade.

Raine crouched down and tried to pick the sword up.

A vision flashed through her mind. She was a little girl. Someone was throwing her into the air and catching her. The wind whipped her hair and strong hands circled her waist. A curly-haired man with warm brown eyes laughed up at her.

He pulled her close and whispered, 'Love conquers all!' in her ear.

Lucky tried to pull the sword from Raine's hands. The vision faded. 'That's amethyst. And the sword's iron. What does it say? Hey, are you alright – you've gone a funny colour.'

Raine collapsed against the tunnel wall. Her knees wobbled and her stomach lurched. 'I feel a bit sick actually.' She rested the heavy sword against the wall next to her.

Johnny put his hand against her brow. She'd almost forgotten he was there; he wasn't normally this quiet. BagDog licked her hand.

'It's the sword, Raine. Iron repels witches. How do you feel now?'

Raine blinked. Her head stopped swimming and the stone floor under her feet stopped rippling. 'Better.' She pointed a shaky finger at the sword. '*That* can repel Morrigan?' She broke into a grin that must reach to her ears.

She grabbed the sword in both hands. It was hot and cold against her skin at the same time. It burned and then froze again and again as her fingers wrapped around it.

'More than that. Iron doesn't just repel witches, it kills them.'

'Where's that rug? I'm taking the sword and I'm going to finish this. For once and for all.' A surge of hot anger followed by a wave of peace washed over her. She staggered against the stone wall. She would have to ignore the feeling. She had a job to do. But there it was, stronger now. Heat bubbled up. It climbed up from her feet to the top of her head. She squirmed.

Johnny stared at her. He reached for the sword.

'No Raine, you don't understand—'

'I do understand! I'm not stupid!' Raine's skin crackled and sparked. Her blood boiled and bubbled, turned to lava and scorched her. Everyone expected her to save the world, but they treated her like a little kid.

She'd show them. She'd kill Morrigan, and anyone else who stood in her way. Then she was going to Skywards to kill Bruiser. Her palms burned. Her hands told her to lift the sword and bring it down on someone's head. *Anyone's* head, it didn't matter who.

Johnny and Lucky shuffled backwards, their eyes so wide and round she could see a circle of white around their irises. Lucky started to cry.

The purple stone pulsed with light. Her fingers glowed violet around the hilt. Raine's hands couldn't be colder if she'd plunged them into a bucket of ice. A chill gushed through her. Her teeth chattered and the tips of her nails frosted over. But she didn't care because the world was beautiful, and she was going to save it. Everyone was going to live happily ever after. All because of her.

'I do understand, Uncle Johnny. The sword is repelling the witch in me, but attracting the daughter of light. It's like I'm fighting myself when I touch it. But I must do this. They need me.' She rubbed her fingers over the amethyst. Johnny and Lucky crept forward, their faces bathed in a purple glow. On the passageway wall, a blurry picture flickered into focus. A forest and a smooth mountain. Tiny moving shapes dotted the mountain's base. The picture zoomed in like a close-up camera. Shrieking filled the tunnel, pummelling their ears. Raine's skin tightened as if it was too small for her body.

They gathered around the flickering image. 'Screechers,' Johnny whispered.

CHAPTER 12
A SACRIFICE

Trees rustled as figures ran and crawled through the undergrowth, swung through the branches, or flitted through the air. Every moment, others arrived to join them. Cackling laughter echoed through the forest. The screams of Screechers filled the night sky.

Raine ran a hand over the tunnel wall. The picture was so clear she could almost feel the heat of sparks from blades being sharpened on rocks fly through the darkness. Arrows whispered through the air before thudding into trees who complained and yelped. Raine wrapped her arms around herself. Her teeth chattered. So, this was the enemy.

Lord Smellott folded his telescope shut and put it back in the pouch slung around his neck. A small voice piped up behind him, 'Can I see? How many are there, Lord?'

The dragon turned his back on the forest. 'Uh, no. My eye glass isn't working properly – no point you looking. Too blurry.' His glance ran over the creatures gathered around the base of the Crystal Mountain. Thousands of armoured and armed Western Dragons stood in ranks on the lower slopes. A few hundred cyclops gathered in loose clans swinging their clubs. The other creatures of light were small and harmless.

Raine's stomach was a stone. They would fight to the death, but it would be a short fight. They were no match for the Dark Army. And it would all be her fault.

Lord Smellott burped a puff of noxious smoke into the air. 'There's about the same number as us! Easily matched and with good on our side – have no fear my friends, we'll succeed, and by morning we'll be celebrating with a victory breakfast!'

Raine's stone stomach sank into her shoes. 'He's lying.'

There was a ragged cheer, and Lord Smellott lied through his teeth, 'I have word the Northern Dwarves are not far and will reach us before nightfall!'

All eyes turned towards the ball of flame that hung low in the sky, barely above the horizon.

'I'm going to get them all killed.' Raine's knuckles shone white around the sword. *Half of me wants to throw it away and never see it again, and half of me never wants to put it down.*

The sun dipped below the horizon. An arrow hurtled from the tree line and stuck in Lord Smellott's shield. He plucked it out and unrolled the piece of paper attached to the end. He unbuckled his sword belt and took off his chain mail vest. He laid them on the ground next to his shield.

'The Sorceress asks to talk,' he told his troops. He walked into the dark woods with his head held high.

'No! She'll kill him! I know she will!' Raine closed her eyes. She hadn't seen Monkey, or Little Thirty-Five, and now Lord Smellott was going to die too. *It's all my fault. I've failed them.* Raine opened her eyes and blinked away stinging tears. She wasn't going to fail them all.

The sun sank from view. Another arrow soared out from the forest. There was a tiny squeak. The first victim of the war had been claimed.

'Right.' Anger and peace fought in Raine's blood. Clammy sweat cooled on her icy brow. She planted her feet, squared her shoulders, and stuck out her chin. She was going to be a warrior princess from now on. What did people say? Fake it 'til you make it?

'I'm off.' Good. She'd hardly sounded frightened at all. She braced her muscles. 'I might cut her head off with this.' She swooshed the sword around her head in a huge arc. It scraped against the stone wall. Sparks pinged in every direction, sending Johnny and Lucky jumping back.

Okay, no. That was too much.

'Sorry,' Raine mumbled. 'Um, Lucky, your beard's smoking.' She pointed to her own chin, nearly slicing it off. 'Whoops. Should've put the sword down first.'

Lucky ran away shrieking and hitting her beard.

Johnny grabbed Raine's shoulder before she could leave. His fingers were like a rock on her shoulder, pinning her in place.

'You're half-witch, Raine.'

'I know.'

'It might kill *you*.'

'Nah.' She was getting good at this sounding brave stuff. Monkey and Little Thirty-Five would be proud.

She stroked the writing on the side of the blade and managed not to cut herself.

'*Omnia Vincit Amor*,' Johnny read. 'Love conquers all.'

Raine grinned. 'Exactly. This was Dad's sword. I'll be fine.' Her mouth twitched; her cheeks ached. Could Johnny tell she was lying? She was either going to get killed by some crazy old witch or by wielding her dad's old sword. But she'd die trying to save the world. The dragons had shown her love and kindness. More than she was used to in her own world. If she didn't at least try and help them, how would she be able to live with herself? She'd made a promise to Little Thirty-Five to help him when they were in the basement together. She wasn't going to let him down now.

***

Standing on a tree stump at the edge of the battleground, a shrouded figure sniggered. The huge snow wolf at her side looked up at the sound. She enjoyed the chaos. She didn't care what happened to her army. This was between her and the girl. If she ever came. Maybe she was a coward, like her mother.

A cloth sack at her feet wriggled. She kicked it until it was still, ignoring the muffled insults that came from inside it.

The battle raged on in the darkness. The creatures of light would be no match for her creatures of darkness. The girl must be too scared to come. Disappointing. It had been ten years since she'd enjoyed a proper fight, and that had only been with Elsie. She had always known she would win, but this was almost too easy. She'd expected Elsie to prepare for this. Had she really thought Morrigan was going to let her get away with banishing her? She should have tried opening the gateway years ago and saved herself a decade of boredom. She'd spent years in this backwater, hunting creatures of light and draining their magic. Once she got hold of the girl's Glimmer, everything would change. Then she'd have enough power to break through all the portals in all the worlds. Everyone knew a young witch's Glimmer was strongest just before the end of childhood. How could Elsie have been stupid enough to let her get so close to the gateway? Morrigan smirked. Her enemies were pushed back towards the Crystal Mountain by her creatures. The largest dragon gave the order to retreat. They were ridiculous creatures, with their absurd sense of honour. Smellott had sacrificed himself so pointlessly. She smiled. He was chained to a tree in the forest, a prize for her Screechers when all this was over.

She would look good in the crown of the Underlands. Morrigan allowed herself one final smile. She and her son would be the new royal family, not only in this world but in the world next to it. Who knew how many other worlds would succumb to her power?

Movement on the mountain caught her eye. Morrigan's smile slid off her face and her hand tightened on the wolf's pelt until he whined in pain. She stopped and stroked his fur smooth. It seemed she would get to fight after all.

She stooped to pick up the sack at her feet and stalked out onto the plain. The time had come for the prophecy to be fulfilled – one way or another, it would be finished.

CHAPTER 6
THE LAST STAND

Raine slid from the hovering carpet. Her feet slipped on the surface of the Crystal Mountain, and she put out a hand to steady herself. A jolt of electricity ran up her arm from the place her father had died. Raine watched his murderer walk out across the moonlit grass of the battlefield. She balled her hands into fists. Her nails dug into her palms. She concentrated on the pain in her hands. It stopped her brain screaming at her to run away.

A hand with sharp nails on Raine's shoulder made her turn. A large, ugly, kind face peered down at her through the gloom.

'This is your time, ducky,' Flo said. 'There's no one else left. It's up to you now.'

'What about Lord Smellott? Is he back?'

Flo shook her head. Her eyes brimmed with tears.

'Little Thirty-Five?'

Flo frowned. 'He's a very naughty little dragon and he's grounded.' She glared at Raine. 'I'd ground you too if I could. Fancy letting him go off with you like that!'

'But did he give you the message? Did he *show* you?' *Please, please, please say yes.* She crossed her fingers.

'I sent him straight to bed with no supper.' Flo folded her wings in front of her chest and burped out two plumes of smoke into Raine's face. 'He'll be the death of me, that one.'

The dragons and cyclopes were running back to the safety of the Crystal Mountain. No Lord Smellott. The witch must have killed him. Poor Smelly. This was her fault. If she'd spent less time getting side-tracked by cyclopes, dwarves and wizards, he'd still be alive.

Little One puffed up the mountain, his blood-stained sword clasped in one great claw. With the other, he wiped away blood from a gash on his forehead. Flo bounded forward, but he pushed her away.

'I'll go with you, Princess!' he wheezed. 'You can't go down there alone!'

Raine shook her head. 'No. Your mum's right. It *is* my time. Morrigan's killed everyone I care about – my dad, Lord Smellott, Monkey. She's not going to kill you.' Raine put a hand on his wing. 'And don't call me Princess. I'm Raine. There's no royal family anymore, just me and I don't think I make a very good princess. But I think I might be quite a good witch.'

She reached behind her head. She pulled the sword from a makeshift scabbard Mrs Battalax had tied from a couple of old leather belts. The sword was too big and heavy for her; she needed two hands to hold it up. It gleamed in the moonlight. Flashes of blue light flickered and crackled along its length. It was like holding a massive, magic sparkler.

'The dwarves made this sword for my father as a gift. When he died Mrs Battalax hid it away. It's probably the only weapon in the Underlands that can kill her.' *And me.* But she wasn't going to tell them that. The last thing she needed was those two getting themselves killed trying to protect her. It was time to take command before they started getting any crazy ideas.

'Little One, who's in charge here?'

'Jesbom. He's missing. He went into the forest to look for Lord Smellott.'

'Little One, I'm putting you in charge. Get everyone up onto the Mountain. As high as you can. Morrigan's army will follow you. You need to make sure the Dark Army is too high up the mountain to escape. They mustn't take shelter in the forest. It's important. Do you understand?'

Little One stood to attention.

'Wait!' Flo reached into a bag slung across her body. 'Put this on, Princess.' She held out a gauzy blue garment that flashed with flecks of silver.

'I haven't got time to put on a party dress, Flo!'

'It's a battledress. Sewn with dragon tears. It will protect you from Morrigan's dark magic. Deflect some of her fire. Not much, but maybe enough to help.'

'Dragon tears?'

'When my husband died, not long after Little Thirty-Five was born, I cried until I was empty. All over my sewing. At least some good will come of it.' Raine squeezed Flo's hand.

'Thank you.' She took her scabbard off and slipped

the dress over the top of her tunic. The material was so fine, it was like wearing a cloud that twinkled with diamond stars. The shimmering skirt fell to just above her knees. Flo helped her put the scabbard on and position the sword on her back.

'Remember – the Dark Army have to be too high to run back down the mountain!' Raine warned.

'But won't they round us up and kill us?' Little One looked extremely pale for a green-faced dragon.

'Do it. Trust me.' Raine squared her shoulders and picked her way down the mountain. She weaved through the exhausted and injured creatures making their way up. She should stop and apologise to them all. She was supposed to look after them and protect them – but she'd been too busy feeling sorry for herself and getting side-tracked.

She'd got her friends killed. She'd put Little Thirty-Five in danger. To be honest, she was a rubbish princess, and it wasn't nearly as fun in real life as it was in stories. If she came out of this alive, she was going to give the Underlands to the creatures of light. They'd do a better job than she would.

But just because she'd turned out to be a rubbish princess, didn't mean she had to be a rubbish witch too. She was pretty sure the sword wanted to kill her, so that must mean she really did have witchy blood. Hopefully also being a creature of light would confuse the sword long enough to keep her alive and finish the job.

Her back burned and froze where the sword rested. That was a good sign, wasn't it? Her witch blood made the sword hot and angry, and her creature of light blood calmed it down.

A swarm of small flying creatures rushed out of the darkness and over Raine's head. One broke away, turned back and dive-bombed her. Raine ducked. Her feet slipped on the glossy crystal slope, and she landed on her bum. *Again? I need to stop falling over. It's not a good look for a hero.*

'Raine!' it squeaked, 'I showed my friends! We can all do it!'

The young dragons flew to Little One, circling around his head.

'Watch this! Look!'

No way! Little Thirty-Five had snuck out, grabbed his friends and then flown back into the heart of the battle. Flo was going to kill him, and Raine.

It was almost funny, death by angry mummy dragon, confused sword or crazy sorceress. Raine sighed. She'd better get on with it. She hauled herself to her feet as Little Thirty-Five presented his bottom to a surprised Little One.

'Watch this!' The row of small dragons lifted their tails and grunted.

Little One lost his eyebrows, but it didn't matter. Little Thirty-Five had bought them a bit of extra time. Raine stepped off the Crystal Mountain and on to the plain.

'To me!' Little One roared.

He dropped to one knee and raised his shield over his head. Dragon warriors sprang forward and joined him – their raised shields forming a wall protecting the smaller animals from a rain of arrows that flew from the tree line.

Arrows bounced off the cyclopes thick skin. One of them dropped with a scream to his knees, his hands clutched around the arrow shaft sticking out from his eye. The cyclopes roared. They charged, leaping over the smaller creatures standing in their way.

A swarm of shadows detached itself from the trees and rushed out to meet the stampeding giants.

Raine clapped her hands over her ears. The clash of metal on metal closed in on her. An arrow whizzed over her head. She ducked and it thudded into the ground behind her.

Little One ordered his dragons forward. With a battle cry, they raced towards the forest. At a shout from Little One, the dragons stopped. They turned to face away from the forest and lifted their tails. The trees caught fire with a whoosh.

Flaming shadows poured out. They screeched and rolled on the ground. Flying shapes burst into the air. They showered the trees with flames, setting more of the forest on fire. The smoke-filled air burned Raine's lungs. The burning trees crackled and the sky glowed orange.

Raine crept out into the field.

***

Raine stopped in the middle of the battlefield. Morrigan stood opposite her, her face shrouded in a hooded cloak. The enormous white wolf, covered in blood, stood by her side. The witch held a brown sack in one hand.

Raine sucked in a deep breath, but the air made her cough. Her eyes streamed. *Great, now Morrigan thinks I'm crying.*

'I thought this was supposed to be you and me? One-on-one.' *Fake it 'til you make it.* 'What's the matter? You scared? Need your friend there to hold your hand?' Did Morrigan notice the wobble in her voice?

Morrigan laughed. An icy finger trailed down Raine's back. 'You have courage, child. In another life, I could have liked you! And as for my friend here.' She stroked the wolf's ears. 'He is my familiar. A witch should always keep her familiar close by. Keep them safe. Surely your mother taught you that, little girl? Here's *yours.*'

Morrigan threw the sack she was holding at Raine. It landed open at her feet. She didn't need to bend down and look any closer to see that Monkey was dead.

Raine battled the wave of anger that surged up inside her. That was what Morrigan wanted. She wouldn't give her the satisfaction.

She looked again at poor Monkey. A wave of sadness washed over her. The sword on her back pulsed through her thin top. It wasn't the hot-cold feeling she'd been getting used to. It was something else. The sword reminded her of her father and the vision she'd had when she'd picked it up. Only she was beginning to think it wasn't a vision; it was a memory. Her dad really had loved her. Knowing that made her stronger.

She kneeled and pulled the sack over Monkey's face. 'I'll cry for you later, my friend.'

Raine stood up straight and tall. 'Show yourself, Witch!

Morrigan pushed her hood back, revealing a beautiful face and long black hair plaited over her shoulder. Raine knew that face. Morrigan was the woman she'd seen in the Scrying Well.

'But... you're... I mean, you're not... an old witch.' Raine's thoughts bounced around inside her head. Morrigan watched, a smug smile twisting her red lips.

'That's right, little girl.' Morrigan smirked. 'I'm Anann. Bardus's wife! I made him fall in love with me, and then I ran away with our son back to my forest! A few blood-stained clothes were all it took to convince him we'd died! Oh, it was so easy to trick the poor fool!' Morrigan giggled and Raine's skin crawled. 'It wasn't long until he came looking for the Sorceress of the forest – and of course, I made sure he found the old crone!'

Morrigan's face rippled. Her hair twisted like a snake. Raine watched her turn into an ancient hag with wiry, grey hair. The old woman cackled.

Her features shifted once more and the beautiful Morrigan stood there again.

'Your idiot mother paved the way for all this. She always was too soft. She should have killed me when she was told! Instead, I get to kill her little girl – fitting revenge for my banishment to this backward world! And once you're gone, the path will be clear for me to become the ruler of the Underlands and Skywards!'

'What about your son? Did you kill him too?' That poor, defenceless baby she had seen in the well's pictures didn't deserve this awful woman for a mother.

'Of course not, fool!' Morrigan bellowed. 'Who do you think will rule when I die? There is a new royal family in the Underlands now, and you will bow down to us before I kill you and take your Glimmer, halfling!' Morrigan advanced on Raine, her arms outstretched, fingers curled like talons. 'You're all that stands in my way, and you're an untrained little girl!'

Morrigan leaped at Raine, knocking her flat on her back. The witch landed on top of her and pinned her to the ground, a bony knee digging into her chest. She wrapped her long fingers around Raine's neck. Morrigan squeezed. Raine grabbed at the fingers circling her throat. Raine gasped for breath and scrabbled at the hard ground. There must be something she could hit Morrigan with. Her fingers raked over grass and dirt.

The sword was useless, strapped to her back and out of reach. Blackness gathered in the corners of her eyes. Her throat swelled; it was like trying to breathe through a straw. She struggled and twisted to break free, but Morrigan was too heavy. Morrigan's grip tightened. Raine wheezed. She couldn't pull another breath. Her lungs were on fire. Raine closed her eyes. She went limp under Morrigan. Her last breath whistled out. The clash of metal and shouting soldiers faded. *This is it. I'm dying.*

A roar erupted from the Crystal Mountain. Morrigan's grasp loosened. Raine sucked in a ragged breath.

Morrigan jumped to her feet. 'What's this? What's happening?' she screamed.

Raine scrambled up, her chest heaving. A stream of furious dwarves poured around the sides of the Crystal Mountain. They roared their battle cry again and pelted on to the battleground. The dwarves, armed with swords and axes, circled the Dark Army –

blocking them from the burning forest. The dwarves started pushing them towards the mountain.

It's working! The dwarves herded the Dark Army, cutting through any of Morrigan's creatures who tried to escape. Screechers poured from the sky, shrieking as they fed on the fallen.

Dark creatures trying to get back to the burning forest were chased and brought down by the cyclops clans, or burned by a fiery dragon's bottom. Little Thirty-Five and his friends zipped through the sky, farting fire and giggling.

Raine faced Morrigan. The witch stood with her mouth hanging open, watching her army fall. The giant white wolf turned and fled.

'Lykoi! Lykoi! Come back! I command it!' the witch wailed. The beast looked over its shoulder at her as it ran for the burning trees. It jumped a flaming bush and disappeared into the darkness.

Raine had to stop Morrigan running back into the woods. She would never be able to find her in there. And who knew what dark magic she could weave from the shelter of the trees? *Anyway, the trees hate me – they'll kill me even if she doesn't.*

'You might as well give up now, Morrigan. You're not powerful enough to stop this. Your magic is too weak! You'll never be anything now! Scurry away like your lap-dog!'

Morrigan swung round to Raine. A red glint danced in her eyes. Her face rippled, dark shadows flickering over her features, twisting back and forth from old hag to beautiful woman.

She snarled at Raine. 'I'm the most powerful sorcerer in the world! They all said Elspeta was the greatest, but I've spent ten years in this backwater with nothing to do but practise!'

Lightning bolts hurtled from the sky and smashed into the ground around Raine's feet. She flinched. Her legs trembled. She wouldn't run away. Not yet. It was all about timing.

'No, you're not!' Raine's voice was too quiet. *I sound like a scared kid, not a warrior princess. I'm not Drippy Raine anymore.* She cleared her raw throat. Her dry lips caught on her teeth, making her snarl back at Morrigan.

'You're a mad, bitter old woman! I'm more powerful than you – I'm a halfling!'

Raine held out her hands. She glared at Morrigan. Cool, blue light coursed through her veins. It glowed under her skin. The sword on her back pulsed with her heartbeat. She pointed her finger and a blue flame shot from her hand.

It pounded into Morrigan's chest. The witch crashed to the grounds. Sparks flew from the evil witch's hair as she scrambled back to her feet.

Morrigan flung a red lightning bolt at Raine. Raine skipped sideways. The lightning bolt scorched her cheek. It exploded on the ground by her feet.

'I'll kill you!' Morrigan spat. 'I'll kill you! I'll cut out your heart!'

She hurled another bolt at her. Raine ducked.

Another lightning bolt hurtled at her. She jumped into the air. It burned through her trousers. Pain shot up her leg. She staggered but stayed standing. *Don't look. I'll be fine.*

The book smacked against her thigh.

The book! EM and MM! Of course! No wonder Morrigan was so angry. And now, Raine was going to make her even angrier. She had to get the witch away from the forest.

Raine pointed at Morrigan. Blue flame burst from her finger. It shot straight past Morrigan and hit a passing troll.

Whoops. Raine looked along her arm like she was looking down the barrel of a gun. She took aim. The blue flame hit the plait hanging over Morrigan's shoulder. The stink of burning hair filled the air. It was nearly as bad as Little Thirty-Five's burps.

The newly bald Morrigan hissed at Raine. A forked tongue slid out between her lips. Raine smiled. Not even Bruiser had ever looked this angry.

Raine stuck her tongue out at the furious sorceress. Then she turned and ran. She sprinted towards the Crystal Mountain. Lightning bolts exploded at her heels, making her run hop. She peeked over her shoulder. Morrigan was at her heels, hurling red fire as she ran.

Raine stumbled. The heavy sword tipped her forward. She tripped over her own feet and fell. She curled up into a tight ball and squeezed her eyes shut.

A pair of hands reached down and grabbed Raine's shoulders, lifting her off the ground. Her saviour galloped towards the mountain, with Raine bouncing over their shoulder. Black, tangled hair whipped Raine's face and got in her mouth. *Tantu!*

'Thank you!' Raine coughed, spitting out hair. 'She was going to kill me!'

'Think nothing of it, Princess.' Tantu wheezed. She jumped over a dragon in chainmail lying on the grass. Raine's chin slammed into Tantu's shoulder.

'Tantu, you can see! But that means...?'

Tantu's pace slowed. 'He's gone. His journey has ended.'

Raine and the cyclops reached the base of the Crystal Mountain. Tantu put her feet on its glossy slope and charged up.

A scorching ball slammed into Raine's back. Tantu staggered and dropped to her knees. Raine tumbled from her back. Her head smashed into the mountain's surface. Darkness seeped into the edges of her vision. Not again. She shook her head, but that made it hurt even more. She closed her eyes. Much better.

Something pulsed against Raine's back, digging in and uncomfortable. She wanted it to stop. Her bed would be much more comfortable if whatever it was would let her go to sleep. She wriggled. Worse. She opened an eye.

Raine rolled. A fork of lightning smashed into the mountain beside her. She rose to one knee, pulling the sword from its scabbard as she moved. Morrigan ran up the mountain. Her movements were disjointed and jerky, like she was sharing her body with a spider. Raine's stomach rose to her throat.

Raine lurched to her feet. She slipped on the

smooth, glassy surface. Her feet shuffled. She skidded, the heavy sword knocking her off balance. She fell and started sliding down the mountain on her back. She clawed at the slick crystal. It was like trying to grab a mirror. Morrigan stopped running and laughed. Raine picked up speed. She rocketed past a green blur in an apron. Morrigan cackled.

Raine held the sword out to her side. Its weight shifted and her slide changed direction. She crashed into Morrigan. They rolled down the mountain together in a thrashing tangle of arms and legs. Two strong, green arms finally brought them to a halt.

Little One pulled his claws from Raine's dragon tears dress. It was torn from neck to shoulder and her trousers were half bunt off. Her leg stung and her hands hurt. She didn't care. She had Morrigan right where she wanted. She patted her thigh. Her bag was safe.

They scrambled up. Morrigan and Raine glared at each other. Morrigan hissed. Her eyes were red slits. Morrigan tossed a flaming red ball up and down in her hand.

'I'll kill you,' she snarled, 'you little *beast!*'

Raine grinned at Morrigan. She leaned on the sword hilt, pushing the blade into Morrigan's foot.

She didn't stop until she felt the tip dig into the mountain.

Morrigan gripped the hilt.

'Ow!' she screeched, letting go of the sword. She blew on her hands. Smoke poured from her injured foot. It smelt like burned matches and rotten meat. 'That really hurts!' she whined.

Same. Raine ached all over. How much worse would it be if Flo hadn't made her battledress? Her back throbbed. At least the sword had stopped trying to kill her. Morrigan's foot was turning black.

Does my back look like that?

She was so tired. Even if she had won, her friends were dead. And her dad. All because of Morrigan.

Black strands crept up Morrigan's leg. She tried to make a ball of lightning. She managed to summon a small, glowing coal. She tossed it at Raine. It bounced off her shoulder and fizzled out on the ground.

Really? You're still trying to kill me?

'Why are you so horrible?' she yelled at Morrigan. 'You're my aunt, and you should be nice! I don't want to kill you, but I'll have to because you won't stop being so nasty!'

Morrigan stopped hissing. She blinked and her

eyes turned human.

'Elspeta told you?'

'No. I worked it out.' Raine opened the bag and pulled out her book. She held it up. '*EM* and *MM*. You and Mum. Elsie and Morrigan Major—'

'Magicka. Elspeta and Morrigan Magicka. Daughters of the First Family. Keepers of the Lore.'

'Why do you hate Mum so much?' Tears burned her eyes. 'Why do you hate me?'

Black tendrils curled around Morrigan's neck. 'I'm jealous,' she said. 'Elspeta was always our father's favourite. He was going to make her the Grande Dame, even though I'm the oldest.' Morrigan hung her bald head. 'I'm sorry.' Black strands crept across her cheek.

The ground shuddered under Raine's feet. She struggled to balance on the slippery slope. Cracks spiderwebbed the white crystal under Morrigan's feet. Their eyes met.

'The sword,' they said together.

The mountain groaned. A long, jagged crack zigzagged under the point of the sword. It raced towards Raine. The crack widened. Raine jumped to the side. Her foot slid and she slipped backwards.

A hand shot out and grabbed her by the wrist. Morrigan yanked her away from the edge.

Raine and Morrigan clung to each other on the edge of a crevice. Raine reached down and, ignoring her burning hands, pulled the sword out of Morrigan's foot. She hurled it into the mountain. It cartwheeled into the darkness. Her hands smarted. An icy tingle crept over the burning.

'I'm so tired, Aunt.' Raine's eyelids fluttered. Her knees buckled.

Morrigan held Raine up. 'Ssshh, little one. Time to sleep.'

'I'm not Little One, I'm—' Raine slumped in her aunt's arms. She could sleep forever.

She reached up with a hand that weighed a hundred pounds to flap at an insect buzzing around her head.

'Go 'way,' she mumbled, 'gotta go sleep.' The insect batted her face.

'Urgh. So 'nnoying.' A disgusting smell reached up into her nostrils. Her eyes flickered open.

Little Thirty-Five bobbed up and down, smacking her cheek with his wing. It was irritating, but not enough to keep her awake. Morrigan reached out to grab him. Her face wasn't black anymore and her hair had grown back. She looked young and pretty. Raine floated off again. It was nice having such a loving aunty. She couldn't wait to take her home. After she'd had a snooze. Little Thirty-Five zoomed away, hovering over the chasm. Raine's eyes drifted shut.

'She's stealing your colours!' he peeped. 'Wake up!'

Raine yanked her heavy eyelids open. All around her flashes of rainbow light exploded in the air. They showered down over Morrigan and Raine. The colours bounced off Raine and climbed up Morrigan, twisting around her body and sliding into her skin.

'So beautiful,' Raine muttered. 'Like fireworks.' She'd have a proper look after she'd had a little nap. She was just going to shut her eyes for a minute or two first.

A needle in her cheek made her eyes spring open. She slapped a hand up to her face.

'Little Thirty-Five!' she howled. 'What did you do that for?'

He danced up and down in front of her face, his tiny talon outstretched. 'I'll do it again if you don't stay awake! That lady's taking your colours away!'

Morrigan's hand connected with Little Thirty-Five. She swiped him away.

'Ignore that little brat. Sleep.' She stroked Raine's hair. *It feels like Mum.* Raine rested her head against Morrigan's chest. She was so comfortable. A bit more rest would be nice. The rainbow flashed in the darkness behind her eyes. She floated away in a sea of colours.

Bony fingers circled Raine's ankle and squeezed. Long fingernails dug into her skin. Her foot slid towards the chasm. She was pulled from Morrigan's arms.

Raine's eyes snapped open. She was wide awake. A thin hand had emerged from the crevice and gripped her ankle. It dragged her towards the gaping hole. Morrigan grabbed on to the back of Raine's tunic and yanked. Another hand appeared and threw Raine's sword out of the mountain. It landed with a clang at Raine's feet.

CHAPTER 14
THE MAN IN THE MOUNTAIN

Abig, green figure barrelled down the mountain, sending anyone in its way flying, and pushed Raine aside. Flo reached into the hole and heaved. A man sprawled onto the Crystal Mountain. The creatures of light dropped to their knees. Morrigan lay panting on the ground, her hair in a heap beside her. Colour poured from her and spread in a pool across the crystal. Raine lay next to her, colours puddling under her. It was like lying in a bath of warm jelly.

'I knew you couldn't be dead! I knew it!' Flo trilled, patting the man's hairy cheeks. His breath came in shuddering gulps.

Raine sat up. She groaned. Her hand found the sword. It glowed when she touched it. Her fingertips tingled. The blade sparked with blue light.

Love conquers all.

It couldn't be. Could it?

The man raised his head. His scruffy hair reached to his waist, as did the shaggy beard that covered half of his face. His clothes were in tatters and bleached a pale grey. He sat up and looked around him.

'Thanks, Flo, knew I could rely on you,' he croaked. He licked his cracked lips. 'I'd do anything for a cup of your betelnut tea!'

The man staggered to his feet. He wobbled over to Morrigan. He raised a foot to kick her, swayed and fell over. He slapped her bald head instead.

'Witch!' he sneered.

'Prince!' Morrigan spat, 'I knew I should have killed you!'

'You took me from everyone I loved!' the man rasped. 'My wife and my little girl. Ten years I've been stuck in that mountain. It was worse than death.'

'I'll kill you now to make up for it!' Morrigan sprang to her feet. She raised her hands. Red fire dance along her outstretched arms.

Raine raced towards Morrigan. She leaped in front of the man, thrusting the sword out. Morrigan's fire bounced off the blade and ricocheted back at her. It smacked Morrigan in the face and she flew backwards with a squeal. She disappeared, shrieking, into the gloom of the mountain.

The man and Raine lay tangled together on the mountain. She pushed herself up.

'Hello D—'

'Down!' the man screamed, pushing her against the ground. He threw himself on top of her. A shape soared out of the mountain. It growled. Flames spewed from its mouth. Raine's hair crackled. A wave of heat rolled over them.

Raine peered out from under the man. The creature crouched. Its lion's mouth opened wide and roared while its serpent tail flicked from side to side. It sprang and swiped the man with a massive paw. He slumped bleeding to the ground. Raine wriggled out from under him. Flo dashed over and cradled his head in her arms.

Raine and the creature faced each other. She must look a sight. Her clothes were torn and burned, she'd lost a shoe and her hair would be a frizzy cloud like usual.

I don't care. I'm me. Not a princess, and not Drippy Raine. I'm Raine.

Her Glimmer surged along her veins. Not the cooling blue light or the hot, angry red but a rainbow – perfectly balanced. She patted her bag. It didn't matter that the book didn't help anymore. *I know what to do.*

Her hand slipped inside the bag. 'Morrigan Magicka!' she called. 'You'll never beat me!'

The beast pounced. Raine flung Lucky's coins into its flaming mouth. The bag burst into flames, leaving a pile of money melting on the creature's tongue. The molten coins poured down its throat.

The chimera collapsed to the ground. It coughed and crumpled on its side. Silvery lead dribbled from its mouth. The creature wheezed and shuddered. It pulled itself by its claws to the edge of the chasm. It rolled and disappeared inside the mountain.

Raine stumbled over to the crevice. She lay her hands on the flat surface and breathed deeply. She blew. A rainbow poured from her mouth and down the inside of the mountain. It flowed over the edges and rolled down the slope. Raine finally closed her mouth and the gap shut with a snap. The mountain was smooth and glossy, shining in the moonlight.

A hand gripped her shoulder. 'Raine?'

She turned. 'Dad!'

***

Having a dad wasn't turning out like Raine had expected. He was very nice and everything, but they were arguing already. She rolled her eyes. *Why don't grown-ups ever listen?*

Clarus stroked her hand. 'I can't leave, sweetheart. They need me.'

Raine kicked her feet under the pink bedclothes. Flo had insisted she get into bed the minute they got back to the Hive for a proper rest and a nice cup of tea.

'They don't need you! The dragons were doing a great job. *I* need you. We can finally be a proper family.'

The man whose face she'd seen in the well, and in her vision in the tunnel, looked old and tired. At least he'd had a bath and trimmed his beard, but his new clothes hung off his bony shoulders.

He lay next to Raine on Flo's bed and propped a pillow behind his back. The dragon family stared down at them from the rows of portraits on the wall.

She put her head on his shoulder. He smelt like soap and laundry powder.

'I've waited so long for this,' he said into her hair.

He held her hands between his own.

'I have to stay here. And you must go home. To your mum.'

'But...' Raine's stomach flipped. 'I've only just found you!'

'I know. But I can't go Skywards – I'm King and my place is here.'

'But Morrigan's dead!' Butterflies fluttered in her stomach. Something wasn't right, but what? 'I killed her, Dad.'

Raine's hands shook. She'd killed her own aunt without a second thought. What sort of person did that make her? What if she was a bad witch like Morrigan? She needed to speak to Mum, who had *a lot* of explaining, and a bit of kicking Bruiser out, to do.

Her father shook his head. 'There are other Dark Ones in the worlds.'

Yeah, like me, cold-blooded killers. She was too hot, and Flo had tucked the bedcovers in too tight. Her palms were sticky in her dad's hands.

'I have to stay here and make sure nothing like this ever happens again.'

'Well, then I'll stay here! We'll get Mum, and we'll all live here. Together!' Raine's mouth pulled downwards. The answer was in his eyes.

'No, I'm sorry, my love. Neither of you can live here.'

'But you don't understand! Mum's a witch!'

'There are rules, which must be followed. Your mother called it *the lore*. We broke those rules because we fell in love. I know she's a witch. I always did. We never kept secrets from each other, only from the rest of the worlds.'

'We should change the rules. You can resign—'

'You mean renounce the throne. I can't do that.'

Raine traced the outline of a flower on the bedspread with her finger. It wasn't fair, any of it. The dragons had done a brilliant job of ruling the Underlands for the past ten years. Much better than Clarus and Bardus had managed, who'd both abandoned the throne. *What was the point in any of it, if life was going to go back to normal?*

'It won't go back to normal.'

Raine frowned. So, Dad could read her thoughts

too, like Smelly and Monkey. She snorted. She missed them.

Clarus handed her a tissue. 'Banishing her sister was the last magic Elspeta ever used, against the Lorekeepers' explicit orders. And look what happened. She's not free to come here, and you must return home to be taught properly.'

He gave her a final squeeze and reached over to where her red suit lay, clean and mended.

'Come.' Clarus smiled at Raine, but the corners of his mouth trembled. He sniffed. It was his manners she'd inherited. She sniffed back at him.

'Your mother would not be impressed. Now get dressed. We owe your army a celebration.'

A loud knock rattled the door. A brown, furry face peered around it.

'Can we come in?'

'Monkey!' Raine laughed as he hurtled into her arms. 'I thought you were dead!' She scratched behind his ears. The animal wriggled with pleasure.

Monkey jerked his head at the door. '*He* fixed me right up. Just like that.' He clicked his fingers, but his stumpy, furry paws didn't make any sound.

Uncle Johnny stood leaning against the door

frame. A small man in a robe stood by his side. He looked a bit like Clarus. The statue by the well, Lord Duro. She'd been right, he was alive.

Johnny's fat cheeks shook as he rushed over to the bed. BagDog leaped onto the bed and started licking her face.

Johnny beamed down at her 'Well done, lass! You showed that uppity witch who's boss now.'

Another knock at the door made Raine look up. A shaggy white-whiskered face peered around the door. Little Thirty-Five sat on his head.

'Smelly! I thought you were dead too!'

Little Thirty-Five buzzed up to the bed. 'Watch this, Raine!' He inhaled and breathed out a long, orange flame. Clarus's eyebrows went up in smoke.

'I need to practise my aim!' Little Thirty-Five squeaked, flapping around her head.

Raine had her best friend back and her father by her side. She should have been happy. The worlds were saved, her friends were all alive, and so was her father and his cousin, Lord Duro. But she was as miserable as she'd been back home. She'd found her father, only now to lose him! But there was nothing she could do. Dad was right; Mum couldn't live in the Underlands, and there was no way Raine was leaving her Skywards, alone with Bruiser. She was going to go up there and kick him straight through the gateway. Or she might turn him into a frog.

She was going to have to be brave and enjoy every moment she had with Dad. But she'd find a way, somehow, for them all to be together. Even if she had to go and find the Grand Magus and make him change the lore.

She smiled to herself. *What's the point of being a halfling if you can't do things your own way?*

EPILOGUE

The fires had died down, and the Army of Light lay strewn around the great hall where they'd fallen, gently snoring. Candles sputtered on the walls, flickering over the scraps of a feast. The band slouched over their instruments on the stage, too tired to look up as Raine, Clarus, and Uncle Johnny rose from the high table and stepped over slumbering bodies as they tip-toed to a dark doorway. Raine scooped a sleeping Monkey from where he was curled up on Flo's tummy. Raine smiled. Flo and Smelly had fallen asleep holding hands.

Little One bowed his head. The golden saddle on his back gleamed in the torchlight. Monkey scurried up Little One's side and settled onto the saddle. Johnny puffed and pulled until he too had climbed up.

Raine clung to her dad.

Johnny reached down and, their hands holding onto each other until the last moment, her dad passed her onto the dragon's back. She leaned down from the saddle. Her tears splashed on her dad's upturned face.

'Will I see you again, Dad?' she whispered.

He blinked back the tears in his own eyes. 'It is my fondest wish, Daughter.' He kissed her goodbye.

Little One flapped his great wings and rose from the floor. Watching her father shrink smaller as they circled upwards, a thought niggled at Raine's brain. Had she forgotten something important? So much had happened, it was all a blur. The memory skipped and danced out of reach.

They rose through the slumbering Hive, and as they were about to break through to the open sky Raine hung over the side as far as she dared and shouted down to the figure standing below.

'Her son!' she yelled, 'Morrigan has a son! Another halfling!'

The King waved. Had he heard her?

They dove into the clouds and headed for the Gateway.

Shawline Publishing Group Pty Ltd
www.shawlinepublishing.com.au

SHAWLINE
PUBLISHING
GROUP

More great Shawline titles can be found by scanning the QR code below.
New titles also available through Books@Home Pty Ltd.
Subscribe today at www.booksathome.com.au or scan the QR code below.